Simon's Challenge

"... the plot is unfolded with great liveliness and credible dialogue."
Times Literary Supplement

"We never lose sight of the real challenge of the title — the family's determination to survive as a family ..."
Times Educational Supplement

"... vivid and realistic ... the story moves along crisply ... a tale well told."
Children's Books

Theresa Breslin

Simon's Challenge

Kelpies

Kelpies is an imprint of Floris Books

First published in 1988 by Blackie and Son Ltd
First published in Kelpies in 1989
Published in 2002 by Floris Books
Copyright © 1988 Theresa Breslin

The publisher acknowledges a Lottery grant
from the Scottish Arts Council towards the
publication of this series.

British Library CIP Data available

ISBN 0–86315–408-5

Printed in Europe

This book is for Tom, Patricia, Kathleen, Caroline and, of course, John.

1

Simon kicked the cot moodily. Hands in his pockets, he looked down at the sleeping baby. He kicked the cot again harder. The baby burped and a small curdle of milk escaped from the side of her mouth.

"Simon," his mother called from the kitchen. "Is Jessica awake?"

"No," Simon called back. "But I could arrange it," he added under his breath. He took his hands out of his pockets, rested his arms on the cot rail and looked down at Jessica. Actually, as sisters went, Jessica was OK, he thought. The reason he was discontented was because his mother had, for the umpteenth time, been unpersuaded to buy a computer. She was unmoved by his arguments and pleas. He had explained to her how humiliating it was to be the only person in his class, possibly in the whole of Scotland, not to own one. He had pointed out the educational advantages which owning one would have for both her children and how it would make her own life much easier. The answer was still no.

"No debt, Simon," she always said, "no debt. Your dad's still away looking for work and we have to be careful. We will save up and buy one."

Save up! Simon groaned. By the time they had saved up enough money he would be an old man and too far gone to appreciate anything.

The baby blew a bubble in her sleep. Simon smiled at her. He had been rather disappointed when Jessica was born, since he had convinced himself that the baby was going to be a boy. A lot of his friends had sisters, most of them older than Jessica, and the stories he heard of the

problems that sisters would create made him realize
how lucky he was. With Jessica being so young he felt
he had a distinct advantage. He would have the opportunity to train her properly right from the start. She
would learn about important things like handling frogs
or model planes very gently and not chucking them
about like Guthrie's sister did. There were very few
sensible girls about; he would ensure that she was one
of them. Most especially she would not whisper or gig-
gle with silly friends. Guthrie, his best friend, had the
worst sister of all time. She was his twin, and for some
reason she thought this made her his equal. Guthrie's
mother had told him confidentially, however, that he
had been born twenty minutes before his sister.

Guthrie's full name was Horatio Nelson Guthrie.
Everyone, including Mrs Davies their teacher, called
him Guthrie. Only his mother insisted on calling him
Horatio. Quite obviously Mrs Guthrie had been suffer-
ing from postnatal depression when she had picked
names for her children. She had called her twins
Horatio Nelson, and Hibiscus Mary. It was a medical
fact that mothers could behave strangely after they
had given birth; Simon had read up on this when his
own mother was expecting Jessica. He had carried
dozens of mothercare books backwards and forwards
to the library for her. It had said in one of these that
after the birth a mother could burst into tears and display uncharacteristic tendencies. And he had pointed
this bit out to his dad: "Husbands should try to be
more understanding and helpful and try not to be jeal-
ous of the new baby." His dad had laughed. In fact,
Simon remembered his dad used to laugh a lot. A big
man, with hair which wouldn't lie flat when he combed
it (a bit like Simon's own), he would throw back his
head and shout with laughter.

Simon sighed. He leaned over into the cot and touched the baby's ear. Then he straightened up. He would go and see Guthrie, he thought, and persuade him to come out for a while.

He went downstairs, hands in his pockets, jumping on each alternate stair. He went through the kitchen and out the back door.

"Where are you going?" he heard his mother call.

"Guthrie's house for an hour," he shouted back, timing his shout to coincide with the slam of the door.

He decided on a shortcut through next door's garden. This was risky. Their neighbour, old Mrs McPhee, was always complaining to Simon's mother that he trampled her flowers and ate her fruit. This was untrue. Simon had a special game he played when crossing her garden, and was particularly careful to leave no trace of passage. He climbed the fence, slowly raised himself to eye level and surveyed the enemy territory. The pillbox kitchen windows looked empty; the path was clear. Washing hung damply on the line (they were grazing cows). Nothing else moved.

"Safe to proceed, my old friend." He said farewell to the guide who had led him to the border. He was on his own now. One last bit of open ground to cross before freedom.

"Advance with caution," he whispered. Alien MakFee who controlled this part of the border was a person of devilish cunning. The path was probably heavily mined — better to avoid it. He was halfway over the fence when the back door opened and Mrs McPhee hobbled out to take in her washing. One of Alien MakFee's patrol tanks! Simon dropped like a cat into a foxhole on the other side and crept along behind the raspberry canes. He took some nourishment as he went; it had been weeks since his rations had gone.

The turret of the tank swivelled slowly; he lay flat on the ground; it moved on. He got up. It swivelled back. He would have to make a run for it. The gun lowered to catch him in its sights. He raced for the opposite wall. Up and over as the shell was fired. The wall still vibrated with the impact as Simon sauntered down the lane on the other side, whistling to himself.

Simon's mother watched him from the kitchen window. She shook her head, and reached for a tea towel. That boy really needs his father back, she thought as she began slowly to dry the dishes. It was nearly six months since Joe had been at home. Supposedly he was looking for work up North. She sighed, knowing that Joe was just glad to get away from tensions created by little money and no prospects. Funny how they had stuck together through the struggle when there had been a glimmer of hope that the steel works might be saved. The fight had seemed to bond people together, united in one effort. Then came the awful realization that it wasn't going to happen — there would be no reprieve. A life of school clothing grants and Social Security giros stretched ahead of them.

Upstairs Jessica began to wail.

2

Simon crossed the open ground at the end of the lane and made a detour past the shopping precinct to check that his computer was still there. The window of the electrical shop gleamed at him. Whenever Simon went shopping with his mother she always stopped at the baby shop; her face would soften at the rows of little bootees, the pink smocked dresses and the crisp broderie anglaise petticoats. Simon would go straight to Peterson's whose window was crammed with every conceivable electronic device. Calculators were propped up in their polystyrene cases; black and chrome radios sat smartly on top of their boxes; sleek black padded earphones and small fluffy headsets were arranged down each side of the window. Every type of digital watch, some with functions which even Simon could not understand, was placed along the front of the window; while in the middle, in pride of place, was his computer. He gazed at it longingly. He knew the publicity printout by heart.

Superb picture quality. Menu driven for ease of use. High resolution graphics ... and (the part which he had pointed out to his mother) ... a whole new way to learn ... sharpen your children's maths, spelling and reading skills ... educational software available.

A small notice on one side said "MONTHLY REPAYMENTS AVAILABLE. NO DEPOSIT — INSTANT CREDIT."

He sighed. It was no use, his mother refused to take anything on credit just now. Mr Peterson called over.

"Hey, you're going to wear a hole in my window

gawping at that computer. Here, look what came in today." He held up a computer game. "It's a new version of *Lord of the Rings*. Want to test it for me?"

"Sure, sure, thanks. I mean, yes please."

Simon read through the instruction booklet, then loaded the game and began to play. This was a real challenge. He ran his fingers through his hair and frowned with concentration. He was soon absorbed with Gandalf and Frodo. Someone nudged him. It was Gerry.

"Going to Guthrie's?"

Simon looked up. It was nearly closing time.

"Yeh, hang on."

Simon took the disc out of the machine and handed it back to Mr Peterson.

"Thanks a lot."

"You think I should stock that one?"

"Definitely," said Simon.

Mr Peterson watched the boys cross the car park in front of his shop. They made an odd pair. Gerry was tall with spiky red hair, and his clothes always seemed too small for him. Gangly arms stuck out of his jacket sleeves and his trousers appeared to be at least a couple of centimetres shorter than they should be. Simon, on the other hand, was smaller and darker. He had to stretch his legs to keep up with his friend. His hair was dark and straight and habitually fell over his eyes — serious brown eyes, thought Mr Peterson. A boy who listened when you told him things, a bright boy. He smiled. If he had had a son he would have wanted him to be like Simon, he thought as he carefully locked up his shop.

Guthrie lived in the terraced houses a few streets away. The horrible Hibiscus was sitting on the front doorstep playing dolls with a friend.

"I've been up all night with Matilda. She has colic."

Hibiscus spoke in what she imagined to be a mature motherly voice.

"Looks more like leprosy to me," Gerry commented loudly.

Simon sniggered.

"These men have just been to the pub and have no concern for their little children," said Angela, Hibiscus's friend.

Now where did she hear *that*, Mrs Guthrie wondered as she opened the door to let the boys in.

"He's in his room," she said. "Just go on up."

They went upstairs. Guthrie was sprawled out on the floor with his space army around him. Simon and Gerry lay down beside him.

"Your sister gets worse," said Gerry.

"Tell me news," said Guthrie.

An intergalactic war was in progress. An alien vessel had attacked an unarmed interplanetary cargo shop and made off with the cargo after killing two crew members. Federation patrols had witnessed the incident and were in hot pursuit. Guthrie was the alien. He blasted the two Federation Patrol ships to smithereens. Cackling hideously, he made off.

"Eeeeeehhh." He landed on top of his bedside table to refuel.

Simon and Gerry received the alarm call at Military Headquarters. They climbed into their space craft, ignited their nuclear thrust units and gave chase.

"Warp Factor three," Simon instructed his First Officer in a steady voice.

The enemy ship tried to hide in a meteor storm of bedclothes.

"Operate Laser Scanner," commanded Simon crisply.

Guthrie decided to make a run for it. He headed towards the top of the wardrobe.

"Target sighted, deploy Stun Phasers."

Guthrie desperately doubled back.

Through Space they harried the raider, trying at all cost to prevent him reaching the safety of Hyper-Space. Eventually, under Laser fire and with the threat of being blown to atoms, the alien surrendered.

The boys flopped down exhausted.

"You heard from your dad recently?" Guthrie asked Simon.

"Uhuh. He wrote last week. No luck."Simon paused. "Your dad got anything yet?"

"He's doing some gardening and painting, odd things like that."

Guthrie's mother had a job so at least there was some money coming in. They didn't ask about Gerry's dad. He had used all his redundancy money to set up a little business which had gone broke almost at once. Simon's dad had put his "Blood Money", as he called it, into a building society account for when "things got really desperate." They felt sorry for Gerry. His dad hung about the house all day now without getting dressed properly or going out at all. It was something to do with what people called losing your "personal dignity." Guthrie's father seemed more philosophical about the situation. He pottered around the house and garden and got the dinner ready for the family at night. He didn't take being made redundant as a personal insult the way Simon's father had.

Simon remembered what Mrs Davies, their teacher, had said about being made redundant. It was the day after the national news bulletin had stated that Glenburn Steel Works was definitely going to shut down. They had all sat stunned, staring at the TV set.

"I knew it. I knew it," Simon's father said bitterly.

There were very few children out playing that night. The chip and video shops closed early. It was as if the whole area had simultaneously gone into mourning. When they all went into school the next day Mrs Davies was already standing at her desk.

"Pay attention, please, everybody. Simon, would you go and look up this word in the dictionary."

Mrs Davies walked over to the blackboard and chalked up the word "REDUNDANT" in large letters.

"Now, class. *Pay attention!*"

Everyone turned round at once. Mrs Davies seldom shouted.

"I have something to tell you, and I want you to listen carefully. Last night on the national news it was announced that Glenburn Steel Works would in fact close down. I know that you all have fathers, uncles, brothers or cousins who work there, and there is a difficult time ahead. The closure will affect this whole community drastically. Now I am not going to discuss the rights or wrongs of that decision, but there is one thing I would like to say. Simon, read out the definition of the word which is on the blackboard, please."

"Redundant," Simon read out, "surplus to requirements, unnecessary, or superfluous."

"Thank you, Simon. Go and sit down." Mrs Davies turned and pointed to the blackboard. "This word and its meaning applies to things," she said, "not to our workers. Only *things*, that is machines, or the skill to operate them, can become redundant. The world may no longer have any use for the works or the steel it produces, but we always have use for human beings. *People* do not become superfluous. Not even when they are little and helpless as a baby is. We always need each other. We, all of us, have something to give. It is very important indeed that you all understand this. *People are never redundant.*" She looked round the class slowly, at each one of them in turn. "And don't any of you *ever* forget that. Now open your maths books at page twenty-five, please."

Guthrie's father came into the room at this moment.

"Knocking off time, lads," he said. " Better get along home, you two. Your mums have phoned, they want you home now."

Simon and Gerry parted company at the end of the street and Simon set off home through the gathering dusk.

3

Automatically he went home via the precinct. It was
late spring and the evenings were beginning to stretch
out into soft nights. Tonight was chilly. It made your
nose and fingers tingle and reminded you that winter
was only very reluctantly releasing its grip. Simon
stuck his hands in his pockets. He noticed a goods van
on the corner, the driver busily unloading into
Peterson's. It was from quite far away. A "KY" number
(that's Bradford, he thought), it spelled out SKY. He
looked up. Stars were beginning to crowd the blue-
black sky. Pulsing constellations threw their patterns
across space and time. They were all there, seen and
unseen: Andromeda, Antares, Aquarius, Aquila. His
father had taught him all their names. He leaned his
head back further. "Canopus, Castor," he said aloud.

"Cepheus, Cetus, Cygnus." They rolled off his tongue.
"Pegasus, Sagittarius, Scorpius, Sirius." A litany of light
in the sky.

"Watch it, stupid," a rough voice said.

Simon stumbled and nearly fell over. The van driver
had come round the side of his van to get into his cab,
and collided with him. Simon glared at him as the man
pulled the hood of his parka up and drove off.

"That's typical of adults," he thought. "I am standing
here quietly minding my own business, engaged in scientific research. He comes along, doesn't look where he's
going, and I am the one who is stupid."

It was getting late and cold. He headed towards home.

He went into the garden hut first, to have a word with
Jake, his guinea pig. He often had conversations with

Jake. He was reassuring to talk to. For one thing he didn't interrupt all the time, and for another he didn't mind if Simon cried, as he occasionally did when he talked about his father.

Simon was thinking about his father tonight. There was a small hard lump in his chest. Supposing he never came back? Perhaps it would be better to be like Jessica who would remember nothing about him at all. Simon felt panic sometimes when he forgot exactly how bits of his father's face looked, but he felt better when he recalled things like tonight and the stars.

He leaned his arms on the cage roof of the hutch and spoke softly to his guinea pig. His dad had brought Jake as a present for Simon when Jessica was born. Simon knew from the mothercare books that this was probably to avert any sense of loss that he might feel because his mother was no longer giving him, the first-born, all her attention. He opened the hutch door and stuffed some more straw in. The little animal gazed back up at him with adoring unblinking eyes — in much the same way as Jessica did. He had better hurry up or she would have finished her supper and be asleep before he got in.

"Night, Jake," he said as he covered the hutch with the old blanket.

His mother was sitting on the living room couch changing Jessica's nappy. The baby's face lit up when she saw Simon.

"It's a bit late to be out, son," said his mother as he came through the door.

"Yes," replied Simon, "that's why I came home."

She sighed.

"Cocoa?"

"Yes."

"Did you cover up the hutch?"

"Yes."

"Have you done your homework?"

"Yes."

"Did you —"

"Yes."

They both laughed together. She handed him the
baby. He threw her up into the air. She squealed with
excitement. He hugged her fiercely and, putting his
mouth under her ear, made loud snorting noises
against her neck. She screamed and pulled his hair.
She smelled of cream and talcum powder and soft
sweaty baby-smell. He took her to the bottom of the
stairs. She started to crawl up as fast as she could, her
little padded bottom sticking up into the air. He
crawled up beside her, pretending to race her, but let-
ting her reach the top first. He carried her into her
room, dumped her down in the cot and bounced the
mattress up and down. She rolled over and struggled to
sit up. He knelt down beside the cot bars to play at
being a man-eating tiger. He crawled about, growling
and swishing his imaginary tail from side to side.
Jessica watched him, her eyes sparkling. With a sudden roar he flung himself against the bars of the cot.
She shouted, "More! More!"

In the kitchen, Simon's mother glanced at the ceiling and thought how fortunate it was that Mrs McPhee
next door was deaf.

After a bit Simon laid Jessica down, covered her
with her special snuggy sheet and stroked her head for
a while. He put out the main light and, leaving the
small night lamp glowing, went downstairs.

He had his cocoa in the kitchen with his mother.

"Mrs McPhee ..." she began.

He groaned. He had been spotted.

"... is going to babysit tomorrow night."

Simon made a face. The problem was, when his mother went out she liked Simon to come straight home from school and stay in for the whole night. Well, he thought, it might not be too bad. He had a model he wanted to finish making, and there was a lot of fun to be got out of Mrs McPhee. The old lady would never admit to being deaf but she watched people's faces carefully to try to understand what was being said to her. Simon had discovered that if he controlled his expression and shouted key words he could get her to agree to practically anything. For instance, he would smile and shout, "ISN'T IT LOVELY?" Then lower his voice and continued, "Jessica has just thrown up all over THE BEDROOM RUG." He shouted the last three words.

"Yes, dear," Mrs McPhee would smile and nod, fingers busily knitting. "A lovely bedroom rug."

"And," Simon would go on, "IT IS A GOOD thing you're not at home. I can SEE THROUGH THE WINDOW that your house is on fire."

Mrs McPhee agreed. "A good big window to see through."

"I got a letter from your dad this morning," his mother said suddenly.

"Can I read it?"

"Eh, well. It just says really that he hasn't found anything yet, but he'll stay on for a little while longer."

"That's all?" Simon asked.

His mum looked down into her cup.

"Simon," she began. "Simon, your dad's going through a bad patch just now. When people are made redundant they lose more than their jobs; they sometimes lose themselves. Daddy needs some time on his own just now. Can you try to understand that?"

"I'm not stupid," said Simon.

"No, son, I know you're not. Look, go on up to bed now, will you?" Simon went upstairs slowly. He tried to think what it would be like to work in the same job for twenty years and then be made redundant. Perhaps he'd start up a computer business.

He had a quick wash and brushed his teeth, then he lay in bed and planned various torments for Mrs McPhee. Little did he realize that tomorrow's events would put all thoughts of Mrs McPhee out of his head.

4

The next morning Simon and Gerry arrived at the school bus stop together. Lee, a boy in their class whose father owned a Chinese restaurant, was already standing there. Angela and some of her friends were being witty at his expense.

"Ah so," said Angela. "A velly cold day, I tink."

The girls giggled and pushed each other. Lee ignored them. It was easy to look inscrutable if you were Eastern, thought Simon. Lee's face did not colour up the way Gerry's would have at the girls' teasing. Gerry had red hair and freckles, and colour and temper would flare at once in his face if he thought that anyone was making fun of him. For this reason the girls loved baiting him and had nicknamed him "Ginger Gerry." They must have started on Lee as he was the first and only boy at the bus stop this morning.

Angela bowed low. "What have you got in your lunch box, Honourable Gentleman? Number twenty-four or number fifty-two?"

Simon glared at her. Lee was not a special friend of his but against the common enemy the boys closed ranks.

"The Chinese are one of the oldest civilizations in the world, and we had to learn from them. They had laws and writing when the Picts were still painting themselves blue," Simon lectured her. "They had great philosophers and knew how to make paper. And fireworks," he added.

"Yeh, they had good ideas," said Gerry, "like how to keep girls in their proper place, by binding their feet for instance."

The bus approached the stop. Lee suddenly drew himself up. He stretched his arm straight out and, pointing at Angela, he chanted something in Chinese. The girls gaped at him, for once at a loss for a reply.

"What was that?" asked Simon.

"An ancient Chinese curse," Lee said solemnly. He consulted his watch. "In approximately forty-five seconds her ears will rot and fall off."

The boys fell about laughing, while Angela tossed her head huffily. Her ears were rather large and stuck out slightly.

Gerry pretended to inspect them.

"Could only be an improvement."

The bus drew up and they all piled on. As they made their way up the passageway Angela suddenly screamed and fell across a seat clutching her ears. She rolled about in agony.

"The pain, the pain. Make it stop, please make it stop." She rubbed her ears frantically.

Everybody looked at Lee and then at Angela who was now writhing on the floor. Bedlam broke out.

"Make it stop," shrieked Hibiscus and started to cry.

The driver stood up.

"You kids sit down at once or you'll walk today."

Simon looked at Lee.

"What did you say to her?"

"Nothing, I mean it was a joke; it was a recipe for soup." He didn't appear very confident.

The driver started to walk towards the back of the bus. Angela stood up immediately, brushed the dust from her skirt and quickly sat down beside her friends.

"You boys *sit down* or I'll report you," yelled the driver.

The boys stamped up to the back of the bus.

Angela tossed her head.

"Gullible," she said loudly.

"Simple Simon," chanted Hibiscus. "Simple Simon."

Her friends joined in, laughing hysterically. "Simple Simon, Simple Simon."

The bus pulled away from the stop and went out of the estate along the main road. Simon liked this part of the journey best. There was still quite a bit of open country between their houses and the school. On a cold morning like today, with the rising sun still low in the sky, the hoar frost clung to the leaves and lay like a velvet mat on the fields. It reminded Simon of the story of the Snow Queen which he had read to Jessica. Although unable to understand, she had listened intently, the poetry of the words compelling her to quiet.

Now they were passing the silent steel works. There was a big sign which said, "Glenburn Cold Reduction Mill" and then a board across this which read "Closed." Someone had sprayed "R.I.P. Scotland" in black paint over it. When his father was on early shift Simon used to walk up the road after school to meet him coming out of the works gate. The men were always joking and calling to each other, or standing about in groups talking and arguing while waiting for the bus. Once his father needed to recheck a piece of machinery and had taken Simon inside. He had explained how the hot-rolled steel they received was processed into cold-rolled coils and sheets which were used for things like washing machines, fridges and office furniture; much went abroad for use in cars in European factories. The huge rollers in the tandem mill could reduce the steel to a thickness of .25mm and work at speeds of sixty-four kilometres per hour. Great coils of steel were moved about with travelling gantry cranes. His dad had told him that to keep the boilers

running the works drew over twenty million litres of
water each week from the nearby Monklands Canal.
By the time Simon had walked back out into the sun,
the vastness of the mill and the life throb of the huge
plant had left him feeling humble and shaken.

He was jerked forward suddenly in his seat as the
bus stopped at the school gate.

5

The class project for this term was "The Romans." Everybody loved this particular project. Mrs Davies would let them play out Roman campaigns in Britain. The boys would be the Roman soldiers armed with rulers as short swords. The girls, the barbarians attacking them from the hills by jumping from their chairs. Guthrie had managed to kill his twin this way on several occasions. At the moment Simon's group were constructing a model of the eruption of Vesuvius, and he was making some small figures. Some were fleeing Pompeii, others had stopped to loot the shops and were falling to the ground choking in the terrible sulphur fumes. He allowed a mother and small child to escape by placing them carefully on a slope away from the lava flow.

"Well, you'll never get your computer now," said Guthrie. He was doing the lava advancing on the doomed town. Personally Simon thought he was overdoing it — half the place was buried. Guthrie always went to extremes.

"What do you mean?"

"Didn't you hear — Peterson's was done last night. They cleared the place out. They must have had some nerve. Old man Peterson always goes back to the shop after supper and they'd been and gone."

Simon could hardly believe it. A robbery only minutes away from his own house and he hadn't heard anything.

The bell went for lunch break and the boys took their sandwiches to a quiet spot in the playground away from the Infant School kids. It never ceased to

amaze Simon the way the Primary Ones and Twos all
charged about at break times, yelling and banging into
each other, without being able to organize a proper
game. He supposed he must have been the same himself at that age. Simon bit into his apple. He was glad
his mum made him a packed lunch. A lot of his pals
went "Free Dinners" now, but it was something he
would have hated to have to do. The boys discussed the
robbery.

"They think it might be terrorists," said Guthrie
confidently. Guthrie's mother worked at the police station and he always had the latest news on the crime
front. Not always accurate, Simon had discovered in
the past. Guthrie tended to fill in any missing details
from his own imagination.

"That's garbage," said Gerry. "What would terrorists want with Peterson's computers?"

"Well, an organized gang anyway," Guthrie said
huffily. "There's a few places like Peterson's been done
over the last couple of months. They're real profession-
als, never leave a trace, and they must have somewhere to get rid of the stuff. That has all the hallmarks
of an international operation."

"But not terrorists," persisted Gerry. "You made
that bit up."

"What about the serial numbers," said Simon
quickly to avert a row.

"Easy, they file them off."

"Don't the police have any clues at all?"

"Old man Peterson has still to give them a list of
everything that's been taken. My mum saw him at the
station this morning and she said he looked terrible, as
if he'd had a heart attack or something. He'll probably
never reopen. They were like children to him, you
know, those computers." Guthrie was quoting his

mother again, thought Simon.

He wondered what he would do if someone approached him and offered to sell him a computer very cheaply. He would arrange to meet and have plain-clothes policemen scattered about. He could be wired for sound and lead them on to make enough incriminating remarks before the trap was sprung. Or perhaps it would be better if he and his friends handled it themselves. He thought of different ways they could arrange this.

"Where were the other shops that got stuff stolen?" asked Gerry.

"All over," Guthrie said. "North of England, Midlands, this bit of Scotland, but not any real pattern to it, my mum said."

The children who went home for lunch had started to filter back through the gates. Simon screwed his sandwich bag up into a ball and threw it into a group of girls playing ropes. Suddenly John McDougall, a boy in Primary Six who had gone home for lunch and lived right opposite the steel works, came rushing into the playground. His face was bright red and he was out of breath with running so fast.

"The cats!" he shouted. "The cats! They're killing all the cats."

6

John McDougall was soon surrounded by a crowd of children all talking at once. Gerry grabbed his arm.

"What are you saying?" he asked. "What cats, where?"

"Up at the works. They're rounding them all up with big nets and bags and taking them away to be gassed."

"Let's go and take a look," said Simon.

Leaving school premises without permission even during lunchtime was forbidden. Only those children who lived close enough to the school to have lunch at home were allowed out. However, this was obviously an emergency situation and the boys gave no thought to school rules as they raced up the road towards the works. The main gates were closed but they soon found a way in, and, running more slowly now, they went round the side of the main building.

It was true. Several vans with "Glenburn District Council — Pest Control" written on their sides were drawn up at strategic points around the yard. They were there to keep down the rats and had been fed with scraps from the canteen. He noticed Mr Patrick, the local vet, standing beside one van. He knew him quite well as he often took Jake down to his surgery to get his nails clipped. Simon went over to him.

"What's going on?"

The vet looked up. He had been setting out some fish in a large cage-like contraption.

"Simon? Isn't it? You shouldn't really be here." He looked at the boys' faces. "The cats will have to be put down. It is the only thing to do. They're too wild to be taken as house pets and if we left them they would starve to death slowly. Honestly, boys, it's for the best. They don't feel a thing."

Already from all corners cats of different sizes and colours were appearing, lured by the pungent smell of fish. They crept forward warily towards the traps. Old fighting toms and battle-scarred tabbies with little kittens following, hunger making them lose their usual caution.

Simon suddenly felt sick.

"I'm going back," he said. "The bell's going to ring soon anyway."

The boys turned and wandered disconsolately back down towards the school. Guthrie viciously kicked a tin can which had been lying inoffensively by the side of the road.

"I'm fed up with this place," he said.

Nobody answered him. In the distance they heard the school bell and by force of habit began to hurry along.

The news spread quickly through the school. Even the teachers were talking about it. It was a very subdued class that Mrs Davies struggled to teach that afternoon.

The time passed slowly. Simon slouched across his desk. He thought of his computer; the prospect of owning one faded still further. Probably when Mr Peterson got his new stock in, it would be much dearer. Yet a computer was the one thing that Simon had really wanted. All other things were nothing compared to this. He would have given up his pocket money forever if only ... He thought of Mr Peterson. The old man would be very upset. He loved all electrical gadgets and didn't mind when Simon came in to look round on his way home from school. He was always eager to show how things worked and now and then would allow

Simon to set up the demonstration discs. What if he did give up his business? Everybody round here was giving up on everything.

Mrs Davies shut the book she had been dictating from with a loud snap.

"Right, I think we all need cheering up this afternoon, don't you? Pack all books away in your bags and no homework this weekend. Let's get the painting materials out. Turn your desks towards the window. You can paint what you see out there." Their classroom looked out on to the football pitch, with fields beyond.

"Look across there," she went on. "The lambs are out with their ewes in the farmer's fields, and do you see the trees along the edge of the field? The rooks are starting to make their nests. They are building high up in the branches this spring. That is a sign of good summer weather to come."

Some of the class groaned.

"Or you can paint from memory," she went on. "Come on now. I want to see some Da Vincis or Vincent van Goghs."

She went about filling empty yoghurt cartons with water and giving out brushes and paints.

"Paint something exciting that has happened to you recently." She chattered on, trying to lift the gloom that hung over the children. She opened the window.

"There, that's better, some fresh air to blow away the cobwebs," she said brightly.

Simon drew a cage, and then a cat sitting beside it. He changed it and made the cat enormous with huge fangs and put a small man cowering with fear beside it. He stabbed angrily at the paper with his paintbrush. He outlined a van, a white van. He stood back and looked at his painting. He saw a cat, and a van with a man standing beside it. A man beside a van.

A van. *The* van. THE VAN! Simon gripped his brush. Last night! That van, at Peterson's when he had gone home via the precinct. It wasn't new stock arriving. The man hadn't been *un*loading, he had been *loading* into his van. He was the thief. And I saw him, thought Simon. I stood there and watched him taking my computer away. He nearly shouted out in the class. He would have to tell the police. He, Simon, might have the very clue they were looking for. He thought about telling Guthrie and Gerry. Better to leave them out at this stage in case he had made a mistake. He came to a decision. He would check with the police first about the time of the robbery, and then he would know for sure if the van he had seen could possibly be involved.

He could hardly wait for the lesson to end. He tried desperately not to glance at his watch.

"Simon Ross, stop looking at your watch all the time," said Mrs Davies. "If you don't want to paint any more, you can take these books back to the library before the bell rings."

The bell rang.

Simon grabbed his bag and the books and raced for the door. He flew down the corridor into the library.

"Returns from Primary Seven, slips inside the books, Mrs Davies says 'thank you very much.'" He slammed the books down in front of an astonished Miss Hendry and seconds later he was in the playground.

He skirted the crowd at the bus stop and shouted to Guthrie. "Don't hold the bus for me, I've something to do tonight."

As he approached the Glenburn police station he slowed down. His heart was thumping. I must be calm, he thought; I don't want to make a fool of myself. He went slowly up the steps.

7

Outside the door of the police station Simon hesitated for a second, and then, swinging his schoolbag over his shoulder, he marched straight in. He walked up to the counter.

"Hello, sonny, lost, are we?" the desk sergeant said jovially.

Simon ignored this.

"I have reason to believe that I may have some information which may be of value to the police in certain inquiries they are making."

"Oh yes, and what would that be then?" The officer leaned across the desk.

"That," said Simon, remembering the 'sonny,' "I will divulge to someone in the Detective Division. I can tell you, however, that it concerns the raid on Peterson's last night."

The police sergeant looked at Simon for a moment or two.

"This is not a kid-on?"

"No," said Simon firmly.

"Right, come this way then." And he ushered Simon through a door marked "Interview Room." He went out. Simon looked around him. The room was very bare, furnished only with a table and two chairs. There were no pictures on the wall. Simon wondered how many criminals had been broken in this very room. The door opened and a man came in, accompanied by a woman in police uniform.

"Hello," said the man. "I am Detective Inspector Harrison and this is WPC Forbes." He smiled helpfully at Simon.

Simon cleared his throat. "Before I begin," he said, "I would like to make a phone call."

"A phone call?" said the Detective Inspector.

"I am entitled to make one phone call," said Simon patiently.

The detective and the WPC exchanged glances.

"Eh, certainly," said Detective Inspector Harrison. "WPC Forbes, would you fetch this gentleman a telephone, please?" He turned back to Simon. "Would you mind telling me just who you intend to call?"

"My mother," said Simon. He coughed. "She, er, becomes concerned if I am a few minutes late." He hesitated. The man had a nice face. "Since my father went away she has become very anxious about me."

"I see. Where did your dad go, son?"

"Up North, to see if he could get on the rigs. He used to be an engineer in the steel works. He lost his job when it closed down."

"Aye, so did half the town," said Detective Inspector Harrison under his breath.

"So you see," continued Simon, "I have a lot of responsibilities at the moment."

The WPC returned with a telephone and pushed the lead into the wall socket.

"Excuse me," said Simon and made his call.

His mother did not seem to be appreciating his thoughtfulness in calling her. Simon held the receiver away from his ear.

"I particularly asked you to come home early tonight. What are you doing in a police station?" Her voice was getting higher and higher. "Who is with you?"

The detective signalled to Simon to give him the phone.

"Do not be alarmed, Mrs Ross," he said. "Your son

may be able to help us. He might have seen something last night near Peterson's shop which was broken into and goods taken. Please do not worry. I personally will bring him home safe and well shortly." After speaking for a few more minutes he put the phone down.

"Are you carrying a gun?" asked Simon.

"Gun? Eh, no."

"I would be prepared to be hypnotized," said Simon.

"Hypnotized?" Detective Inspector Harrison looked blank.

"Yes. People will remember details under hypnosis which they might not otherwise recall." Simon was beginning to have serious doubts about this detective's capabilities. The man kept repeating everything he said and did not seem to be familiar with basic police procedure.

"I think we'll leave that for the moment," said Detective Inspector Harrison, "and go over exactly what happened last night. Just tell us in your own words what you saw and did."

He listened without interruption while Simon described his movements of the previous evening. Then WPC Forbes, who had been taking notes, read back everything he had said.

"You say you bumped into the man. Can you describe him?"

Simon realized to his dismay that he could in fact remember very little. He didn't know what the man was wearing and he was unsure now of the colour of the van.

"This often happens," said WPC Forbes while Detective Inspector Harrison was out of the room. "It will come back to you later when you are not thinking about it."

Detective Inspector Harrison had returned with

folders which contained pictures of different types of
vans and sketches of men of every description. Simon
looked through them. It was hopeless. His mind was
empty. Nothing familiar to him. Detective Inspector
Harrison stood up.

"We will stop now and I will run you home."

"I did see someone loading a van," Simon said
desperately.

The WPC gave him a friendly smile.

"We believe you," she said. "If you had been making
it up you would have given us more information than
you actually have done. The best thing to do over the
weekend is to try *not* to think about it."

Simon was embarrassed. She is being kind because
I'm stupid, he thought as he walked out to Detective
Inspector Harrison's car. They rode home through the
teatime traffic snarl.

"Pity this isn't a proper police car," said Simon.
"Then you could have turned on the siren and passed
all this lot."

"Oh I can arrange that," came the reply. "You
deserve to get home in time for dinner after all the
effort you've made trying to help us."

Detective Inspector Harrison opened the glove com-
partment and took out a light fitment with a cable on
it.

"The base is magnetized," he said.

He reached up and out of the driver's window and
attached the light to the roof of the car.

"The cable is connected to the car battery."

He flicked a switch. The light began to flash and the
piercing note of a siren sounded. Immediately cars in
front began to pull into the side of the road. Detective
Inspector Harrison put his foot down and their car
accelerated away quickly. They were home in minutes.

When they turned into his street Simon could see his mother at the front door anxiously watching for him. Detective Inspector Harrison hurriedly turned off the siren.

Simon went into the kitchen to have his dinner. Jessica was in her high chair banging a spoon on the tray. Simon could hear his mother and Detective Inspector Harrison's conversation in the hall.

"There is no doubt your son saw something which may be of importance. The time ties up exactly with that of the robbery. I would like to see him again after the weekend if that is all right with you. We think this may be part of a bigger operation. Meanwhile he should try to put it right out of his mind."

They were talking about Mr Peterson now.

"Yes, it was quite a shock for him. He's well covered by insurance of course, but a thing like that, it is bound to affect him."

Mrs Ross saw him to the door.

"I'll be in touch. Bye, Simon," he shouted.

"Next time, Simon," his mother said as she came into the kitchen, "please tell me *before* you do anything like that again. My nerves can't stand it." She sat down to have a cup of tea with him. "What's wrong?"

"I feel sure that there is more in here," he pressed the side of his head.

"Well, you would be better to do as they advise and forget it for the present."

"I suppose so." And Simon resolved to try to put the matter out of his mind for the weekend.

8

Around seven o'clock Mrs McPhee came over and Simon's mother went downstairs to give her instructions. Simon followed her down into the living room. He couldn't concentrate on his model-making tonight.

"Could you put a night nappy on the baby at eight o'clock and give her a drink of milk, please?" his mother was yelling at Mrs McPhee. "Simon doesn't need to go to bed early, tomorrow's Saturday."

Mrs McPhee nodded and smiled.

"Right, see you later, Simon." She knelt down in front of the baby. "Bye-bye, ma wee darlin'."

Jessica looked uncertain and her lip trembled.

"Oh, oh, Simon," his mother said.

"I'll take her on to the front lawn for a bit," said Simon.

"OK. It's a beautiful evening, but don't let her stay out too long in case she gets a chill."

Mrs McPhee came out and sat at the front door to keep an eye on Jessica while Mrs Ross slipped quietly out the back door.

Simon sat on the grass and made Jessica a daisy chain. He put it round her neck. Then he brought Jake out of the hut and let him explore the wild undergrowth below the hedge. The street was busy with children playing. As the light nights came in at this time of year the sunset was delayed longer each evening. The earth spun slowly past its equinox and children everywhere behaved in accordance with the same elemental forces. Ritual games dictated by season were started up spontaneously everywhere. Hopscotch was chalked out in patterns handed down from older sisters. The sounds in the street were those which had echoed in town gardens and tenement courts for generations.

Mrs McPhee sat Jessica on her knee and started to play with her.

"Two little dicky birds sitting on the wall,
One named Peter, one named Paul ... "

Simon remembered her doing this with him when he was small. He never could work out how she made the two little pieces of paper which she had stuck to her forefingers disappear so quickly. It had been ages before he knew that it was her middle fingers that she took out from behind her back.

"... Fly away Peter. Fly away Paul ..."

Jessica watched fascinated.

"Come back Peter. Come back Paul."

While Mrs McPhee was changing Jessica, Simon made some supper for them both. The phone rang as he was buttering the toast. Maybe it was the police station calling to see if he had remembered anything.

"Good evening," said Simon. "This is the Ross residence, Simon Ross speaking. Who is that calling please?"

There was a silence.

"Simon, is that you?" It was his dad's voice.

"Oh, hello, dad. Where are you? How are you getting on? Have you got a job yet?"

"Simon, what are you playing at, answering the phone like that?"

"I'm expecting a call from the police station."

"The *police*? Is everything all right? What's the matter? Let me speak to your mother."

"Calm down, calm down. Everything's fine. Mum's

gone out tonight. Mrs McPhee is here looking after us, or rather I am looking after her," Simon added. He told his father everything that had happened.

"That's a shame for Mr Peterson," said Simon's dad. "I hope he doesn't pack it in. The town is going to need shops if it's going to stay alive."

There was a pause in the conversation.

"When are you coming home, dad?"

"I don't know yet. I'm travelling around a bit to see if there are any better prospects anywhere else. Look, take a note of this number. You can get me here if you need me. And," he added, "tell your mum I called."

The pips went and they were cut off. Simon hung up and carried the tray through to the living room. Adults are most peculiar, he thought. He took Jessica from Mrs McPhee and carried her up to bed.

"Down and out," he said firmly. "There's a film on telly I want to see." He tucked her up and left her.

Later, when he was in his own bed, the day's events came crowding back to disturb his rest. He saw wild cats chasing escaping criminals. He was in a police car, the siren screeching; he glanced to his right and saw that Mrs McPhee was at the wheel.

"Don't worry," she said. "I'll remember where we're going in a minute."

They pulled out to overtake — she must have been doing ninety miles an hour. She started to sing in a loud voice.

"Two little dicky birds, two little dicky birds sat upon a wall."

As they drew alongside the robber's van Simon could see the driver's face quite clearly. It was his father.

A noise downstairs made him wake with a start. He

listened. It was only his mother saying goodnight to Mrs McPhee. He heard her come upstairs to go to bed. She looked in on him.

"Dad phoned," he whispered.

"Yes, I saw your note on the hall table."

"He said to tell you he was asking for you."

His mother smiled at him.

"Good night, Simon."

"Good night, mum."

Simon turned over and went to sleep.

9

"Come on, lazy bones," his mother was shaking him awake. "I thought you wanted to go to the library this morning?"

"Uuuuh." Simon buried his head further into the bedclothes. He had been in the middle of a particularly good dream.

"Go away."

"It's nearly half past ten and we've got to go to the shops."

"Right, OK. I'll get up in a minute."

"Don't believe you. So I'm about to use my ultimate weapon. And, believe me, this morning she is the *ultimate*."

His mother pulled back the duvet and sat Jessica down on his chest.

"I'm going downstairs to make the breakfast. I'll expect you two in fifteen minutes, washed and dressed."

The baby bounced up and down on Simon's chest, gurgling happily. A horrible smell was coming from her nappy.

"Whew, Jessica, how could you?"

He carried her into the bathroom and stood her in the bath while he undressed her. Then he took down the shower head and sluiced her off.

"You're disgusting."

She laughed and clapped her hands. He squirted some water in her face. He let her play about while he got himself washed and dressed, then he wrapped her in a bath towel and carried her into her room to find her clean clothes. This was the tricky bit. Unless you kept a firm hold of the squirming bundle she would escape and it could take upwards of twenty minutes to recapture and dress her. He held her tightly as he put her nappy on and rammed arms and legs into vest, socks, trousers and jumper.

Then he sat her on his knee and put on her little shoes. Jessica was very proud of these, despite the fact that she could only walk a couple of steps without falling over. Simon lifted her onto his shoulders and took her down into the kitchen where he sat her in her high chair. Mum was making fried potato scones, bacon and eggs. He realized that he was starving.

"That was a dirty trick," he said.

"You're telling me." She piled his plate up and set out a boiled egg and little bread soldiers on Jessica's tray.

Simon looked out the library books and strapped Jessica into her buggy while his mother got ready.

They took the bus from the precinct to Glenburn town centre and went across the park to the library. Simon picked a space adventure book, one nursery book to read to Jessica and two books on the Romans. At the library desk there was a leaflet on sale with a colour-in poster about the Romans. His mother bought this for him. Mrs Davies had told them that Glenburn was the site of one of the Roman forts on the Antonine Wall, which stretched across Scotland from the River Forth in the east to the Clyde in the west, and kept back the wild Caledonian tribes from raiding the Lowlands of Scotland. Remains of the fort had been found in the park, and the finds had included sandals, pottery, lamps and weapons. Less than a hundred years ago a leather bag with fifty Roman coins in it had been discovered near the bandstand. For days after this piece of news, the park had been infested with boys from Simon's class digging among the flower beds, until eventually the Parks Department had complained to the school and the Head had forbidden any school pupils to go near the park for a month. However, any time he was in the park Simon always kept a sharp eye out for interesting objects.

He was doing this now as they came out of the library and went towards the swings. Simon really admired the Romans, despite the fact they had conquered his ancestors. That had only been for a short time anyway. The military engineers who had laid out the defensive system of the Antonine Wall must have been very skilful. The roadway on which the armies of Rome had marched was protected by a rampart over three and a half metres high and on the other side by a massive ditch. At Glenburn the ditch was hewn out of the rock by captive labourers cutting across the face of the hill to a depth of about three metres. At this part of the wall there was an uninterrupted view across the Kelvin valley to the Kilsyth and Campsie Hills. There had been about seven thousand men manning the wall. The legion here had earlier been stationed on the Mount of Olives, and had taken part in the siege and capture of Jerusalem. There had been a cohort of Syrian archers. Simon shivered in the breeze as he pushed Jessica down the hill to the swings. How cold they must have felt, in their short tunics, far away from their sunny homeland in this northern outpost of a vast empire.

Buds were beginning to open on a huge tree of spreading May blossom beside the swings, and rows and rows of daffodils along the border of the path. Last term Mrs Davies had made them learn a poem about daffodils. Simon thought it was pretty awful, something about fluttering in the breeze and your heart dancing with the daffodils. Poems about flowers were boring but they had done one about poppies that was good. It wasn't really a flower poem, though — it was a poem from the First World War, about poppies growing in the fields of Flanders, and how bright the red colour showed among the gravestones of the dead soldiers.

They ate cheese sandwiches and drank juice sitting on the grass, then they set off for the shops and the weekly market.

10

The market was crowded with stalls all vying with each other to attract custom. The Pakistani traders always had the brightest-coloured stalls. They sold embroidered tops and fringed skirts in vivid purple, gold and green. Bright bolts of cloth lay one on the other, all colours of the spectrum. You could buy anything here, footware and food, ironmongery and second-hand goods. Simon got his pocket money and went towards the second-hand section. His mother stopped to buy fruit.

"You're not so busy today," she said to the man, who had tossed three apples into a brown bag and was deftly twisting the corners closed.

"Not the same money about, hen," he peeled the skin from a small banana and handed it to Jessica.

"Say 'thank you,'" said her mum.

Jessica stuffed the banana straight into her mouth. Everybody laughed.

Simon didn't know what to spend his money on today. He had offered to take a cut in his pocket money when his dad had lost his job. His mum had laughed and said, "We're not at that stage yet, I hope."

Normally at this time of year he would be buying fishing tackle, spinners and floats. He wandered past the stall that sold these things. There wasn't any point. He had always gone fishing with his father on the upper reaches of the burn which had given the town its name. There it formed a small loch, and they had camped there, just the two of them, a couple of summers ago. He mooched around among the bric-a-brac and junk until his mother came over with two plastic carriers full of shopping.

"Here, Simon, lend a hand."

Squally rain clouds were beginning to form in the sky as they made their way along the main street to the bus stop.

"I don't see why dad had to sell the car." The shopping bags were beginning to weigh heavily on Simon's arm.

"We couldn't afford that last repair. We have to think long term." Simon's mother stopped to put the rain cover on the buggy. "Mind you, we could be doing with it just now."

The rain came on heavily as they stood in a huddle in the bus shelter with some other people from the estate.

"I heard the police brought your boy home last night," a voice behind them said. Simon and his mother turned round. It was nosy Mrs Boyce from the end of their street. Simon's dad always said that she had asked for the end house specially so that she could keep her eye on everyone's comings and goings.

"Did you?" said Simon's mother and she turned back and pretended to be fixing something on the buggy.

"The lad'll run wild, right enough, with your man being away?" Mrs Boyce said this last part as a question.

Simon saw his mother's face going red.

Please don't say anything, he prayed silently. Don't answer her.

"If you lift out Jessica, I'll fold up the buggy," he said loudly to his mother.

Mrs Boyce was not to be put off.

"Here let me help you, dear. It's such a nuisance to be trammelled with all this stuff when you don't have a car."

Simon saw his mother gritting her teeth. He gritted his teeth.

Make the bus come, he prayed.

The bus came. Mrs Ross snatched her bags from a startled Mrs Boyce and with Jessica under one arm struggled onto the bus. She arranged bags, buggy and children around her on the seat so that no one could sit beside her, and stared fixedly out the window all the way back to the precinct. Simon tried to think of medieval tortures suitable for Mrs Boyce. She was further down the bus clacking away to someone else. If she had put his mother into a bad mood, the whole of Saturday evening could be ruined. They usually bought chips from the shop and sat at the living room fire watching TV. They got off the bus at the precinct very slowly, allowing Mrs Boyce plenty of time to get so far ahead of them that they would not have to walk with her.

"Do you want me to go to the chip shop?" said Simon.

"Oh, right, son." His mother unfolded the buggy. "Put the bags in and I'll sit Jessica on top. You can travel home in style tonight," she said to the baby.

Cellino's chip shop was always busy on a Saturday night.

"I hear you saw the robbery, maybe," Mr Cellino said when it was Simon's turn. "See, the way my shop is facing I would not see anybody."

"Two pudding suppers and a bottle of Vimto, please, Mr Cellino," said Simon. "It was Thursday night, that's your early closing so you wouldn't have seen anything anyway. Not that I'm much good either," he added gloomily. "I can't remember enough details to be of any use."

"You'll remember later, maybe."

"Aye, maybe," said Simon.

He went past Peterson's shop. The sightless window

stared blankly out into the dismal night. Was Mr Peterson going to retire as people were saying he would? Simon tucked the chips inside his jacket to keep them hot and, drawing some comfort from their warmth, ran home in the gathering darkness.

He checked Jake quickly while his mother set out the tea things in front of the fire.

"I put the baby right to bed; she was exhausted," she said as Simon came into the living room.

They watched TV for a while, but Simon found he couldn't concentrate.

"You're still thinking of the robbery, aren't you?" his mother asked.

"Mmmm, yes, there must be something I can remember."

"Don't worry, it will come back to you."

That's what everyone says, thought Simon as he went up to bed.

11

On Sunday afternoon, Simon and his family always went over to Granny Campbell's house for tea. Mum bought tobacco for Great-Uncle John and a cake for Granny, even though Granny always sniffed about what she called "shop bought" cakes. Granny Campbell and Great-Uncle John McKay, brother and sister, stayed together in a cottage in the little village of Waterburn a few miles away. On fine days like today the family would take the shortcut across Glenburn Moss and through the cemetery to the village.

The clouds were high in the sky and the wind was blowing in their faces as they started up the path that led onto the Moss. Mum carried the bags and Simon pushed Jessica in the buggy. They kept to the path between the peats, as even in high summer the ground never really dried out completely. Underfoot, the ground was spongy and this had prevented the land ever having been developed for building purposes, a fact for which generations of Glenburn children had reason to be thankful. The place was a natural adventure playground. There were lots of little clumps of thickets which seemed designed for hide-and-seek, gnarled stumpy trees of exactly the right height for small children to climb and make gang huts in, and pools of water near the peats where algae floated and frogs and other interesting creatures lived. People who lived round about cut the peat and used it as garden fertilizer. Simon's dad had tried this too, but despite his efforts (or because of them, his mum had said) their garden would never win any prizes.

Wild flowers grew everywhere on Glenburn Moss: harebells, bluebells, wood anemones and wild roses. Simon had found carnivorous plants, sundew and butterwort and once a wild orchid. In the spring he looked for frog spawn, in the summer the Moss swarmed with children building fires and making dens.

They came off the Moss by the path that led through the graveyard. They usually visited Grandad Campbell's grave on a Sunday, though Granny Campbell would have been already today to leave fresh flowers. Simon left his mother and Jessica beside the grave while he walked up and down the lines reading the gravestones. He quite liked the modern headstones with their gold lettering on shiny black marble, but he much preferred the older part of the cemetery. Here there were stone urns with cloth draped over them and angels with great wings and one finger pointing upwards to heaven. The inscriptions were also more interesting. He went on until he came to his favourite one. This was a huge Clydesdale horse in white stone set on a plinth.

"Sacred to the memory of Archibald Buchanan, who farmed the lands of Acredyke. Born 1824. Died 1922." Simon had worked out that Archibald Buchanan had been ninety-eight years old when he died. He had seen five monarchs on the throne, had lived through the Franco-Prussian War, the Boer War and the First World War, and probably had spoken to someone who had fought at Trafalgar. The inscription on the tombstone was worthy of such a man.

"Our Day is done, Do Thou O God ingather
Safe to Thy harvest-home each wandering one
Leave not one outcast to the tempest, Father,
When Day is done."

"Simon are you coming?" His mother was going out the cemetery gates.

They came down the hill from the cemetery to the little village of Waterburn, spread out before them. It had been a mining village and the coal bing behind it still threw its shadow over the gardens of the houses as once it had over the lives of the villagers. Grandad Campbell had been killed in a pit accident and his wife had gone back to her own family, living in their cottage with her daughter, Simon's mum. Great-Uncle John had never got married or left his family home and he stayed there too. He was a strange, taciturn man. Simon knew that Something Bad had happened to Great-Uncle John during the Second World War when he was fighting in France that had made him this way. It was something the family didn't talk about. His mother explained to Simon that people could get hurt inside and these wounds took longer to heal than those made by bullets. Great-Uncle John didn't speak a lot. This was OK with Simon. It meant that when they were together he didn't have to answer silly questions like the ones other relatives asked him: "How are you getting on at the school now? What's your teacher's name?" Or to put up with silly remarks like, on the occasion he had lost his two front teeth, "Who's been kissing all the girls?"

The cottage was situated in the older part of the village and they walked past the new houses with their identical front doors, gardens and curtains. These had been built long after the coal seams ran out and the pit closed down. They didn't actually belong to the real village and Granny Campbell always referred to the people who lived in them as "incomers." Simon's Granny was old fashioned in many ways. She didn't approve of Simon's mum wearing trousers, and thought of her as still being her little girl. She bossed her about and called her Annie instead of Anne. She scolded Simon but he knew she didn't mean the half of it and he loved her fiercely.

The door of her house when they reached it was, as always, unlocked and Simon walked straight in. He went into the living room where Uncle John was building up the coal fire. He lay down on the rug in front of the fire and started to read the Sunday papers which were lying about. Generations of McKays had read "The Broons" and "Oor Wullie" in front of the hearth. His mum went into the kitchen with Jessica where Granny was taking scones from the oven.

One thing he liked about Granny's, thought Simon, was the smell. There was always something nice cooking or baking and the smell followed you into every corner. There were lots of places to explore, the best being a large walk-in cupboard off the hall. Granny called this "The Glory Hole" and Simon was allowed in to rummage around whenever he wanted. It was full of things which had been in use when his mother's Gran was alive. Last summer they had all gone to the Peoples' Palace in Glasgow and there were similar things there on display. Simon's dad had laughed and teased his mother, saying that she was so old all her childhood mementos were now in museums. There was a great big jelly pan in Granny's cupboard and when he was a little boy Simon had sat in this and pretended to be St Columba sailing to Iona in his coracle.

Simon also liked Granny's front room, although he wasn't allowed in there so often. She had dozens of old jigsaws which she kept in biscuit tins. The jigsaw picture had been cut out and carefully pasted onto the lid. There was a display cabinet with ornaments on it. One was a little Scottie dog which Simon liked especially. It had a

tartan scarf round its neck and a tartan tammy on its
head with the words "A present frae Bonnie Scotland"
written on its brim. There was a Queen Elizabeth II
Coronation tumbler and a George VI Coronation saucer,
and lots of other knick-knacks which Granny sometimes
let him take out and dust very carefully. The walls of the
front room were hung with many photographs of brothers, cousins, aunts and uncles. Most were long since
dead and their children and their children's children
were now citizens of America, Australia, Canada and
Asia. There was a studio picture of Grandad and Granny
Campbell on their wedding day. She was sitting in a
high-backed chair while he stood behind her, his hand
resting on her shoulder. There was one too of Great
Uncle John in his army uniform.

Simon enjoyed looking at the books which were
kept in a glass-fronted cupboard, the door of which
you opened with a little brass key. The children's
books fascinated him. One was called *Sunday
Reading For The Young*. It was dated 1902 and the
illustrations showed boys in sailor suits and girls in
long dresses and pantalettes. The boys were called
"Ned" or "Master Jack" and the stories always told
how wickedness did not pay. His favourite book was
The Boys' Book of Adventure and his favourite story
in it was the story of how Catherine Douglas had used
her arm to bar the door against the traitors who were
seeking to kill King James I of Scotland.

Before tea, Simon gave Uncle John a hand to do some
planting. Already many flowers were blooming in the
garden at the front, bright daffodils, and blood-red tulips.
The catkins were showing and rhododendron heads were
bursting from among their dark green leaves. They
sowed some lettuce and seed potatoes, Simon carefully
mounding up the earth and patting it down the way

Uncle John had shown him. When they stopped for a rest Simon sat on the garden wall and Uncle John took out his pipe and began to fill the bowl. First he cut the tobacco from the block with his knife and then pressed the shreds into the pipe bowl with brown nicotine-stained fingers. He took several minutes to light it with a match, sucking and drawing until he got it just right and the tobacco glowed red. After a bit he spat a long squirt of tobacco juice into the earth beside him.

About six months ago Simon had asked Uncle John if he could have a smoke. Without saying anything Uncle John had wiped the end of the pipe stem and handed it to him. Simon had puffed at it for several minutes before handing it back. He really couldn't see the attraction. It had filled his mouth and nose with smoke which was unpleasant, but it certainly hadn't made him cough and splutter the way you saw people in films doing when they had their first smoke. Shortly afterwards Simon began to feel quite ill. He stood up and the world began to tilt in an alarming manner. Uncle John held his head while he was violently sick into a flower bed. Granny had appeared at the door at this point tut-tutting and scolding.

"Leave the boy be, Maggie McKay," Uncle John had said and she had gone away at once.

Simon had decided then that he would never smoke when he grew up. A few weeks ago in class Mrs Davies had shown them all a picture of a diseased lung and explained how bad smoking was for you. Uncle John probably smoked because of what had happened during the war.

They went back indoors to wash their hands before eating. As they went into the kitchen Simon overheard his mother and Gran talking. It was about his dad.

"He writes every week and phones when he can," his mother was saying.

"Well, you know your own business best," said Gran in a voice which clearly meant that she should take the advice which was now about to be offered.

"Yes," said Simon's mum firmly. "I do. Joe has to have time to sort himself out."

She saw Simon and stood up.

"Come on then, you two, food's ready."

It was curious how his mother always stuck up for his father in front of anyone else, Simon thought. He knew that they had disagreed just before his father had left home. He had heard her say that he would have to face facts and pull himself together and he had said that she didn't really understand.

Simon ate an enormous tea of stovies, bread and butter and home-made scones with Granny's own jam. Jessica was off her food. Granny peered at her closely.

"That wean doesn't look very well to me," she said.

"Rubbish," said Simon's mum. "There's nothing wrong with her. She's not hungry because you"ve been giving her sweets all afternoon and spoiling her." The evening was much cooler, however, and as Jessica was rather listless they decided to take the bus back to Glenburn. They got off at the precinct and Simon saw that Peterson's window was still empty. He went over in his mind the events of Thursday night. Surely there must be something else he could remember?

When they got home, mum put Jessica straight to bed. Simon set out his PE kit for the next day. Then he went to bed too. Perhaps tomorrow Mr Peterson would have some new equipment in and he could help unpack it. He refused to believe that the old man would throw in the towel without a fight.

12

Monday was the worst day of the week, thought Simon, as he shoved books and lunch box into his schoolbag and grumbled about the house, looking for his tie.

"Try under your bed," his mother shouted up the stairs. She was in the kitchen trying to spoon-feed a very unco-operative Jessica. "And hurry up or you'll miss the bus."

Simon eventually located the tie, draped over his mirror. He paused and tried unsuccessfully to brush his hair back. It fell down again, over his eyes. He threw the hairbrush onto his bed and with his blazer half on and his bag over his shoulder he galloped downstairs and out the front door.

"Bye," the crash of the door shook the whole house.

"Good grief," said Mrs Ross as she started to clear up the breakfast dishes.

On the bus, Simon told his story of Friday night's events at the police station. Guthrie's mother had left work before Simon had arrived on Friday night and Guthrie was a bit peeved at being ignorant of the latest developments. Simon took full advantage of this and continuously used phrases like "as I said to Detective Inspector Harrison" or "when the Crime Squad and I were discussing the situation." He riled Guthrie so much that by the time they reached the school he was barely speaking to Simon. It was left to Gerry, usually the hot-headed one, to try to smooth ruffled feathers.

"Will you two chuck it?" he said in exasperation. "We should be helping each other in a situation like this. I've got a great idea. Why don't we act the whole thing out and see if we can jog Simon's memory?"

They did this in the cloakroom while waiting for the bell to ring. A small crowd gathered round them to offer helpful advice. By the time Simon had cannoned into Guthrie (who was acting the part of the criminal) for the third time Guthrie was beginning to lose patience. On the fourth re-enactment he pushed Simon back so violently that he sent him reeling against the coat hooks.

"Oops, sorry, didn't mean to wallop you so hard." He made a big show of dusting Simon off.

"Wait a minute, no don't do that. Wait a minute, wait a minute. That's what happened," said Simon. "The man pushed me and I staggered back." He did it again in slow motion.

Gerry and Guthrie waited expectantly.

Simon shook his head. "I still can't remember anything else."

"Oh for heaven's sake, this is a waste of good playing time before school starts."

The bell rang and they went along to the classroom. The morning lesson was Music. Mrs Davies switched on the radio and the *Time and Tune* programme started. "Today we will study the orchestra. Listen carefully to this ..." Simon's thoughts began to wander.

Had he bumped into the thief or was it the other way around? He knew it was important.

"That was a piece of music called an *overture*," said the radio announcer. "Now, how many instruments could you hear playing?"

"Who can answer that question?" Mrs Davies asked. "Simon?"

"I fell against the van," said Simon without looking up.

The class tittered.

"Simon, I don't know where your attention is this morning but it certainly is not tuned to the music programme."

Just at that moment the door opened and the Headmistress came in.

"Could I have Simon Ross, please, Mrs Davies?" she said. "And," she added, "he won't be back for the remainder of the day."

When Simon got into the corridor, Detective Inspector Harrison was waiting there.

"Hello, Simon," he greeted him cheerfully. "I've got your mother's permission to arrest you for the day. Would you like to accompany me to Divisional Headquarters?"

The headmistress walked with them to the school gates.

"Talented, intelligent, mind of his own," she was saying. With a shock Simon suddenly realized she was talking about him.

As he got into the police car he was aware of a line of curious faces at his classroom window. He tried not to smirk as they drove away.

"We're going to drive to the precinct first," said Detective Inspector Harrison, "and let you walk over the route you took home that night. Then we'll go to Divisional Headquarters. They've got better visual aids than we have at Glenburn."

Simon went round the precinct twice, showing them where the van was parked and where the man was standing. Peterson's shop was empty and dark. Simon tried not to look at it.

They drove to Headquarters in silence.

"Clear everything else out of your head," Detective

Inspector Harrison had said. "School, homework, pals, everything. Now is the time to concentrate. Think of nothing else."

When they got to Headquarters, Simon was taken to a room with a computer terminal. He sat down facing the screen.

"Right, this is you," said the operator. A small figure appeared trotting along a line. "Now here we have an outline of the precinct." He pressed a key. "We've programmed this figure to take the route you took on Thursday night. I'm going to stop you on the screen every few seconds or so and when I do you must tell me what you see in your head at that precise moment. Ready?"

Simon nodded.

"Let's go." The little figure moved jerkily along the screen until Simon himself suddenly called out, "Stop."

"I can see the van," he said. "I mean I remember now. It's white, a white van."

"Are you sure?"

"Yes. It's dirty, but it's definitely a white van."

They played this game several times with Simon sometimes operating the little figure himself. Then they broke off for lunch. Simon had remembered a lot of small details, including the time it had taken him to cross the car park and the fact that he had seen the man before the thief had seen him.

They had something to eat in the staff canteen. Simon loaded up his plate with macaroni cheese, beans and a roll. For dessert he had apple pie and ice cream and added a large glass of Coke to his tray.

"Aren't you having anything?" he asked Detective Inspector Harrison. The detective looked at Simon's tray.

"Er, no, I don't feel very hungry," He took some toast and black coffee over to a table and sat down.

"I think I'll be a policeman when I grow up," said Simon, his mouth full of macaroni. "Except I don't fancy wearing that uniform. I mean they look right wallies in those daft jackets and caps. You don't wear them in the plain-clothes division, do you?"

"Actually, yes, I did wear one at one time, and I suppose I did look a right wally, now that you mention it."

Simon's face went red.

"Sorry. I didn't mean to be rude."

"That's all right, son. Eat up your food and we'll go back to work."

As the afternoon wore on Simon became more and more tired. His brain was going round in circles. They gave the computer a rest and sat and talked for a while.

"I keep trying to remember if I bumped into him or he bumped into me," said Simon. "I feel that it is important but I don't know why it should be."

"Well, let's leave that a minute. You come round here and stand beside me," said Detective Inspector Harrison. "Now, what happened immediately after you collided. Did you put your hand out to defend yourself?"

"No, I couldn't. My hands were in my pockets."

"Did he?"

"No. YES. He did something. I've got it. He pulled the hood of his parka up. His parka. He was wearing a green parka." Simon was getting really excited and talking very quickly.

"Are you sure?"

"I'm positive. I remember because it was unusual as it wasn't raining, yet he pulled the hood up. It must have been to stop me seeing his face. And there is something else." Simon's voice rose with excitement. "Something flashed in the light. It was a watch, no, it was a ring. He was wearing a ring on his finger."

"Which hand?"

Simon thought for a minute. "His left hand."

"Definitely?"

"Yes."

"Terrific!" The two of them were exultant. "We're really making progress."

Detective Inspector Harrison read out all Simon had added to his statement of Friday night and then looked at his watch.

"I think we'll call it a day," he said. "We're both exhausted. I'm going to take you home now. We will try again tomorrow. If you remember anything at all, just phone me."

On the journey home Simon could hardly contain himself. He waited impatiently while his mother and Detective Inspector Harrison exchanged a few words at the door. When she had finished, he burst out with his good news about the amount of information he had recalled.

"So you see," he finished off, "how useful computers are. They are very handy things to have. If it hadn't been for that one I wouldn't have remembered anything."

His mother smiled. "I believe you," she said. "And talking of computers, Mr Peterson phoned today. He said could you go over and see him after tea."

Simon's heart dropped. It would probably be to tell him that he was moving away. The old man had called him up to say goodbye.

13

Simon hurriedly ate up the mince and potatoes his mother had set out for him.

"What's up with her?" he said between mouthfuls.

Jessica's plate was untouched. She would usually copy Simon, eating up her dinner quickly, if a little inaccurately. Food often landed on the floor or in her hair as she waved her spoon about wildly.

"I don't know. She's been a bit peaky all day. Maybe Gran was right and she is sickening for something. Come on, pet," Simon's mum tried to coax her with some milk. The baby turned her head away.

Simon pulled some funny faces which as a rule would start her giggling. He could barely get a smile from her.

"I think I'll give her some Calpol and put her to bed early," said his mother.

Simon went upstairs to get changed. He threw his school uniform over the back of a chair, and put on denims and a sweatshirt. At least he would have no homework tonight, he thought. He had missed that with being at Police Headquarters. It was incredible how this afternoon's talk had refreshed his memory of Thursday night's events. He could see it all so clearly now. The brain was just a computer. All those electronic impulses, those millions of tiny connections at incredible speed which you took for granted. He thought of Jessica eating her dinner. A good ten per cent of it landed on the wall most nights. Her brain hadn't yet developed to the sophisticated level his own had. A person like Leonardo da Vinci must have had a brain which was aeons ahead in evolutionary terms.

He put his hands on each side of his head just above his ears, and stared at himself in the mirror. Somewhere in there was more information. He knew it. It was a case of pressing the right button, like playing *Lord of the Rings*. Finding the signal which would trigger the correct response. He pulled on his jacket. He would retrace his steps again on the way to Peterson's shop.

It was a mild balmy evening with a summery fragrance in the air that promised long hot June days to come. Swallows were swooping and diving above the rooftops. Simon sniffed the air appreciatively. Someone had a bonfire going and the crackle and smell of burning branches filled his nostrils. His spirits lifted. Life was quickening all around him and as his body responded he began to whistle as he ran along the road. He vaulted the small wall that bordered the car park and approached Peterson's from the same direction as he had done on Thursday night. Nothing happened to jog his memory but nonetheless he was confident that it would come — in its own good time.

The shop was still locked up and when Mr Peterson opened the door to him Simon saw at once that there were boxes and crates stacked up behind him. His heart soared.

"You're going to re-open. That's new stock, isn't it?"

"Yes, I am. I telephoned earlier to see if you would be interested in helping me unpack and set up some displays."

"Where do you want me to start?"

"Well, now, I'm thinking of changing everything round. I'll keep the counter where it is, obviously. It would be too much work to move it and it is in a good position anyway. I can see the entrance and all round the shop from here. But say we put the video recorders here along the back wall. And I've branched out a little. I'm going to sell one or two storage units, lower end of the market stuff. Eh, what do you think?"

"I think it's a great idea," said Simon. "You could paint that back wall a really bright colour, maybe red or bottle green."

As he spoke Mr Peterson was opening box lids and pulling out packaging.

"Look," he said, "you open that one there." He pointed to a large flat parcel leaning against the wall.

Simon ripped off the outer coverings.

"Got that in the warehouse this morning."

The parcel contained huge printed cardboard figures. Darth Vader glowered down at Simon. Behind him was the figure of Gandalf, white beard flowing.

"Gosh, they're terrific," said Simon. "You know if you hung them from the ceiling they would look absolutely stunning, especially to anyone coming in the door. Also, you could put a spotlight on them, maybe even use a coloured bulb."

"I knew you would have good ideas, Simon," said Mr Peterson. He was humming happily to himself as he stacked up equipment and ticked off invoices.

"You know," said Simon as he carefully unwrapped the rest of the fantasy figures. "A lot of people thought you were going to give up the ship, retire even. Not me," he added hastily.

"Well," the old man paused, pen in hand. "I must admit I did think about it for a while. It's a strange thing but it wasn't the loss of the actual equipment which affected me most. I was ... it's difficult to explain. ... I was hurt, isn't that stupid?" he spoke slowly. "I took it as a personal affront." He laughed.

"I don't think that's stupid," said Simon loyally.

"Ah well, and then I thought, this won't do. After all,

where will Simon go on a rainy night on his way home from school? I thought I must try again, like Bruce and the spider. Do you know the story, Simon?"

"Oh, yes. We got that ages ago, in Primary Four," said Simon. "It was when King Robert the Bruce was being hunted down, and he was hiding in a cave, and everything seemed hopeless for him. He watched a spider trying to fix its web to the roof, and at last after many failures, it succeeded. Bruce took heart again and he decided to continue to fight to free Scotland. My dad says that he re-created the Scottish nation. He never gave up, even when everything was against him."

"Well, there you are then. The Scots are made of sterling stuff. So ... anyway I heard you may have seen something suspicious on Thursday night. The police told me that you were helping them. Is that true?"

Simon told Mr Peterson all that had happened, dwelling on his time at Police Headquarters.

"I don't feel that I've helped them very much."

"Oh, I am sure you have. They will collect their little pieces together and it will all add up to something bigger. You wait and see. They've probably got one of their main computers sifting through it right now."

They stopped for a rest and had a cup of coffee. Simon sipped the hot liquid and surveyed the chaos around him.

"This place is a real mess," he said.

"Yes, isn't it," said Mr Peterson cheerfully.

Simon watched him bustling about in among the boxes. The old man was really happy. He thought about Gerry's dad sitting around the house all day with nothing to do. As if he had waved a magic wand Gerry's face appeared pressed up against the glass of the shop window. They let him in.

"Wow! Did you get all this off the insurance money?" he asked Mr Peterson.

"Not all of it," said Mr Peterson, laughing. "What do you think of our new look?"

"Oh," said Gerry looking around him, "I suppose it will be OK when you've finished it," he said doubtfully.

"We'll do some more tomorrow, Simon," said Mr Peterson. "I'm going to have a pleasant stroll home, now." He locked up the shop and said goodnight to the boys.

"Want to come along to my house for a bit?" asked Simon.

Gerry's face brightened.

"Yeh."

As they walked home, Gerry asked Simon how he had got on with the police.

"Did they interrogate you?"

"No, I was co-operating with them in their inquiries." Simon explained. "You know the idea you had this morning about re-enacting the incident, well they did that too."

Gerry glowed with pleasure.

"Really?"

"Yes, and on both occasions I felt that there was something important that I was forgetting."

"Well, there's not much more you can do anyway." He put on an American drawl. "Don't worry about a thing, folks, everything's under control, as General Custer said just before the battle of Little Big Horn."

"As the captain of the *Titanic* said just after they hit the iceberg," said Simon.

"As Napoleon said to Josephine on the eve of Waterloo."

"As Edward II said to his troops as they rode towards Bannockburn."

And they went on like this, joking and laughing until they came to Simon's house. There was a strange car parked outside. Simon reconnoitred it carefully. He did not recognize it at all.

"Follow me, Watson," he said. "We will go inside and investigate."

14

The boys could hear the murmur of voices in the living room as they hung their jackets in the hall. Mrs Ross was sitting on the couch talking to the local vet; between them lay a cardboard box. Simon and Gerry looked from one to the other warily. Did this mean trouble? Had the vet come to report that they had been inside the mill on Friday. Mr Patrick stood up.

"I'll be off then, Mrs Ross. How is Jake?" he addressed Simon.

"Fine, fine," said Simon, exchanging glances with Gerry.

While Mrs Ross said goodbye to the vet at the front door, Gerry took the opportunity to whisper, "What's going on?"

Simon shrugged his shoulders. "Search me?"

Mrs Ross came back into the living room.

"Did you know that they had to put down all the cats in the steel mill?" she said. "Mr Patrick was just telling me. Isn't that a shame?"

"Uhuh," said Simon and Gerry together.

"They were far too wild to keep as pets. However, when the pest control people had gone Mr Patrick found this." She opened the lid of the cardboard box. The boys looked inside. Nestling among some straw in the bottom was a kitten. Its eyes were scarcely open and it was making squeaky mewing noises.

"Would you look at that," said Gerry.

"Mr Patrick thought it would be young enough to domesticate. Although I don't know," she said and hastily withdrew her hand as the kitten tried to bite her.

"Can we lift it out? How are we going to feed it?" asked Simon.

"I thought we could try one of Jessica's old feeding bottles. I'll go and warm some milk and see if I can find a teat with a hole big enough."

She went into the kitchen as the boys lifted the kitten out of its box and set it on the couch. It crawled around trying to steady itself enough to stand up.

"It's absolutely beautiful," said Gerry.

Simon's mother came back with the feeding bottle. She tested a few drops on the inside of her wrist, the way she used to for Jessica.

"Right," she handed the bottle to Gerry. "Carry on."

At first Gerry tried to hold the kitten the way he imagined a mother might hold a baby. The milk spilled over his trousers and jumper. Eventually he held the kitten by the scruff of the neck with one hand and jammed the bottle firmly into its mouth with the other. It gulped the milk desperately. Everybody laughed.

"Remember to bring up its wind," said Simon.

Gerry put it down on the carpet. It wobbled around and then sat down suddenly.

"It looks just like Jessica," cried Simon.

"You'll have to give it a name," said Simon's mum.

"You can choose, Gerry," said Simon gallantly.

Gerry thought for a minute. "I'll call him 'Killer.'" He leaned over and spoke to the kitten. "Hello, Killer."

"Ha, ha," said Simon, "look what he thinks of the name you've given him." The kitten had made a puddle on the carpet. Simon hooted with laughter.

"That's it," said his mother, "put your friend in his box and take him up to your room." Gerry and Simon went upstairs. The kitten soon fell asleep in its box, and Gerry started to help Simon with his model building. He was trying to glue a radio mast onto a model ship he was making. Gerry kept going over to the box to check on the kitten. Simon smeared glue onto a matchstick and carefully placed a lifeboat in position.

"Hey," said Gerry suddenly. "Leave that a minute and I'll show you what Guthrie showed me at school this afternoon. Have you got a piece of paper?"

Simon tore a page out of his jotter.

"Read this," said Gerry. He wrote on the paper, "ring," "sing," "fling," "Which part of a bird's body rhymes with all of those words?"

"Wing," said Simon.

"Good, very good," said Gerry. "Now," he rolled the paper up into a tube shape, "extend the pinkie and forefinger of your right hand. Pinkie and forefinger only, please."

"Is this going to hurt?" asked Simon suspiciously.

"There is always a degree of discomfort in any scientific experiment," said Gerry gravely. He very carefully placed one open end of the tube onto Simon's extended pinkie and the other open end onto his forefinger.

"Now please repeat the word you have just told me," he said, "*six times*."

"Wing," said Simon, "wing, wing, wing, wing, wing."

Gerry leaned forward and very solemnly lifted the tube. Holding it in the centre he put one end to his ear and the other to his mouth.

"Hello?" he said. "Who's calling, please?"

The boys fell about, laughing hysterically.

Then Gerry got up. "I'd better go," he said. He went over to the box. "Bye-bye, Killer."

Simon felt a sudden rush of affection for his friend.

"Do you want to take him home and look after him?" he asked Gerry. "I've got Jake, and Jessica. He would still belong to both of us," he added quickly, "but you seem to have the right feeding technique."

Gerry's face glowed. "Do you really mean it?" he asked eagerly.

"Yeh, sure. You take him home tonight. There's some milk left in the bottle. We can get a book on raising cats from the library at the weekend, and we'll split the cost of the food."

"Suits me," said Gerry and lifted the box.

Simon felt a slight pang as he watched Gerry stride off down the path with the box tucked firmly under his arm.

"That was very kind of you, son," said his mother from the kitchen door. "Gerry's not got a lot going for him at the moment. His dad has taken it really bad being out of work."

"You mean mine hasn't," retorted Simon sharply, without thinking.

"Simon!" said his mother.

"Well," said Simon defiantly. "Other people get their act together. Guthrie's dad for instance, and Mr Peterson. I was there tonight and he's talking about modernizing the shop. *He* hasn't given up."

"Your dad hasn't given up either. He just found things a bit of a strain. He was getting very depressed and thought it would be for the best if he was away for a while."

"Well I don't think it's for the best. Nobody consulted me to see what I thought was for the best." He stamped up the stairs to his room, threw his clothes on the floor and put his pyjamas on. "I'm fed up with people making decisions as to what is for the best. Next time *I'd* like to be asked for *my* opinion," he shouted. He was fed up with his father, and his mother as well, he thought. She would use one of Granny Campbell's famous sayings to cover the situation, "We're better off than better folk," or "We're all going the same road, we'll get there in the end."

He lay in bed staring angrily at the ceiling. Mr Peterson had the right idea, he thought. He would go after school tomorrow and help him in the shop. He thought about the robbery and all he had remembered that afternoon. He hadn't even realized he had seen a ring on Thursday night. Yet there was still something else. Something just out of reach that kept slipping away each time his mind tried to grasp it. He fell asleep still wondering what it could be.

15

When Simon woke up it was still dark. He lay for a moment or two trying to remember what had been nagging at the back of his mind. Faint snatches of a dream drifted through his head. Then he heard Jessica coughing in the next room — that must be what had awakened him. He got up and padded softly through to his sister's room. The night light was still burning and as soon as Simon opened the door Jessica sat up in her cot and stretched out her arms to him. Simon smiled and lifted her.

"You're supposed to be sleeping, you wee tinker," he whispered. "Look," he pulled aside the curtain. "All dark, see, everyone's asleep."

He put her back in the cot. She started to cry and held up her arms again.

"Ssshhhhhh! Oh, all right then, just for a little while."

He picked her up and carried her into his own room. He switched on his bedside lamp, got into bed and pulled the duvet snugly round them both. He picked up his book and held it in front of her.

"See, *The Secret Garden*. Now, we've got to the bit where Mary first meets Dickon." He started to read to her quietly.

"It was a very strange thing indeed. She quite caught her breath as she stopped to look at it. A boy was sitting under a tree, with his back against it, playing on a rough wooden pipe. He was a funny-looking boy about twelve years old. He looked very clean and his nose turned up and his cheeks were as red as poppies, and

never had Mistress Mary seen such round and such blue eyes in any boy's face. And on the trunk of the tree he leaned against, a brown squirrel was clinging and watching him, and from behind a bush near by a cock pheasant was delicately stretching his neck to peep out, and quite near him were two rabbits sitting up and sniffing with tremulous noses — and actually it appeared as if they were all drawing near to watch him and listen to the strange, low, little call his pipe seemed to make.

When he saw Mary, he held up his hand and spoke to her in a voice almost as low as and rather like his piping.

"Don't tha' move," he said.

Simon stopped and looked at her. Her eyes were bright. There's no way this baby's going to sleep tonight, he thought. He looked at her more carefully. Her eyes were too bright and she was quite hot. Simon felt wet sweat on his pyjama jacket where she had cuddled against him. She started to cough again. Her breath was wheezy and coarse. He looked at her in alarm. Jessica was sick, very sick.

He went at once and awakened his mother.

"I think there's something wrong with Jessica," he said. "She's not breathing properly."

His mother picked the baby up and felt her head. "I think I'll call the doctor. Simon, you take her, please, and I will go and telephone."

While they waited for the doctor, Simon and his mother got dressed and then sponged Jessica gently and changed her sweat-damp clothes. She had become quite listless and Simon was beginning to worry. Normally after her bath she put up a good fight before anyone could get her clothes back on.

By the time the doctor's car drew up Simon was in a fever of impatience. He opened the front door.

"Hello, and how is young Simon?" Dr McIntyre said and ruffled Simon's hair.

Simon gritted his teeth.

"Jessica is upstairs with my mum," he said. "And will you hurry up," he added under his breath.

They waited while Dr McIntyre examined Jessica. When he had finished he put his stethoscope back in his bag slowly.

"Mmm, a wee touch of something in her chest, Mrs Ross. Quite deep. I think we will pop her into hospital for a couple of days, just to be on the safe side."

Simon gazed at him in horror. Hospital? Jessica in hospital?

"Is it pneumonia?" his mother was asking the doctor.

"No-oo. I don't think so. Look, I'll telephone for an ambulance to come. I would take you myself except I've another couple of calls to make and you would be better in the ambulance. They carry oxygen."

"Oxygen? What is he talking about?" thought Simon. He went over to the cot and picked up Jessica. He took her special snuggy sheet and wrapped it round her, and then, sitting down in a chair, he began to rock her gently backwards and forwards. He heard the doctor telephoning downstairs and then saying goodbye to his mother.

"Just a precaution, not to worry ... Joe still looking for work up North? Well you've got a good one there in Simon. I'll phone the hospital from the surgery tomorrow and see how she is. Try not to be too anxious."

After what seemed an age, the ambulance arrived and the two ambulance men escorted Mrs Ross and Simon, still carrying Jessica, out into the dark night.

One of the men got into the driver's seat while the other came and sat with them in the back.

"Come to your Uncle Frank," he said and made to take the baby from Simon's arms.

Simon gave him a poisonous look and hugged Jessica more tightly to his chest.

Frank looked at Mrs Ross. She shook her head gently. Frank sat down and then proceeded (in Simon's opinion) to make inane conversation all the way to the hospital: "Puir wee sowel," and "The wean will be all right don't you worry," and banal remarks about the weather, until Simon felt like screaming.

When they reached the children's casualty department things began to happen very quickly. A nurse took Jessica, who started to wheeze and cough again, away to be examined by another doctor. Then they were taken to the admission ward and shown into the waiting room.

"Don't you think you should phone dad?" Simon asked his mother.

"I did, back at the house when we were waiting for the ambulance. The hotel porter said he would wake him and tell him."

"I wish he was here, now."

"So do I, Simon," said his mother. "So do I."

I hate hospitals, thought Simon. I hate their horrible smell. It seemed to stink of pain, and people being scrubbed. He tried not to think of what they might be doing to Jessica.

"I'm going to find out what's happening," said Simon's mother.

Simon got up.

"No you wait here, please," she added. She reached out her hand and touched his shoulder gently. "I'll be right back."

Simon sat down and put his head in his hands. The navy blue carpet tiles matched his trainers. His eyes travelled along the floor. There was some paint chipped off the skirting board. He counted the ridges on the radiator from right to left and then from left to right. He studied the posters on the wall. "Protect your child by Immunization," he read. There was a picture of a little girl who had just had a needle stuck into her. He recalled his dad walking the floor one night with Jessica after she had had an injection. I can't bear it, he thought. A terrible coldness was beginning to spread through his body, inside his head, so that he found it difficult to think.

He rested his head against the wall. His mother had been gone a long time. He heard footsteps and opened his eyes again. A man stood in the doorway. He was unkempt and his clothes were scruffy, his face grey and unshaven. They stared at each other.

"Dad!" shouted Simon, and he ran across the room to bury his face in his father's jacket.

16

Simon's dad hugged him tightly.

"How are you, son?"

"Dad, Jessica's sick."

"I know. That's why I'm here." He led Simon over to a bench and they both sat down. "Where's your mum?"

"She's gone to see the doctor."

They waited in the silent hospital, holding each other's hands.

Footsteps sounded along the corridor. Simon's heart began to bump with panic and fear. His mother and a doctor came round the corner. Simon and his father stood up at once.

"Joe," Simon's mother walked forward and then hesitated. "Doctor, this is my husband," she said.

The doctor smiled and shook hands.

"I've just been telling your wife," he said, "your daughter has bronchiolitis. Nothing to worry about. We'll look after her for a couple of days and treat her with antibiotics. In fact, she is already responding to treatment and is fast asleep now."

"I want to see her," said Simon.

"Yes," said his dad.

The doctor looked from one to the other. "Mmm, very well, a quick peep and then home to bed for a rest." He touched Mrs Ross on the arm gently. "All of you," he added. "Have a few hours sleep at home and then come back in."

They went quietly into the ward. Jessica lay on her back in a high-sided cot dressed in a little white hospital nightie. Her face was flushed and her mouth was slightly open but she was breathing much more easily,

Simon thought. His throat was tight with unshed tears. He felt a sudden gratefulness towards the doctors and nurses. To his horror he felt hot tears pricking behind his eyelids. He gulped and rubbed his face fiercely.

"Right, we'll go now," he said.

Mr and Mrs Ross followed him down the corridor and out the main door. The air was cool and fresh. Simon took big gulps of it. He felt quite weak. His mum and dad were standing a little apart from each other.

"How did you get here?" his mother asked.

"I hitched a lift from a lorry driver." There was a pause. "I'll go back in and phone for a taxi."

Simon and his mother sat on the little wall next to the ambulance station. Streaks of dawn were beginning to lighten the sky, and some crazy birds were chirping furiously. Simon's dad came back and sat beside them.

"Ten minutes," he said.

Time passed slowly. Weren't they going to say anything to each other? Simon began to get annoyed. Didn't they know the worry and upset they were causing him? Tonight on top of the last few months was too much for him. Didn't they know how stupid the two of them looked sitting there not speaking to each other?

"Do the two of you know how stupid you look," he burst out suddenly, "sitting there not speaking to each other?"

His father looked at him startled. "What?"

"This whole thing has been a great strain on me," said Simon, "and I'd appreciate it if you two could stop quarrelling and start behaving like grown ups."

"Simon," said his dad, "don't interfere in things you know nothing about. You're just a wee boy."

"No, he's not," said Simon's mother quietly, "not any more, Joe."

"All I know," said Simon wildly and to his dismay he realized tears were pouring down his cheeks. "All I know is that Jessica is sick, you don't have a job, and mum is sad all the time, and I am *fed up*," he shouted.

At that moment the taxi skidded to a halt in front of them.

They got in and Simon wiped his face with his sleeve several times. The three of them sat stiffly in the taxi all the way home. Simon went straight into the living room and took the *Family Health Encyclopaedia* down from the shelf. He looked up bronchiolitis.

"A severe breathing disorder of short duration, caused by a virus which produces inflammation of the smaller bronchial tubes (the bronchioles)," he read. "Common in infants, it responds to treatment very quickly and the patient almost always makes a complete recovery."

Outside he could hear the world waking up. He put the book down. He could hear the hum of the milk float coming along the street, and the sound of the early morning bus screeching to a halt at the end of the road. His mother was standing in the middle of the living room floor. Her eyes were blank. She kept twisting the handle of her bag round and round her fingers. The door opened and Simon's dad came in carrying a tray with three mugs on it.

"I think we should do what the doctor ordered and try to get some rest. Everybody drink this up and then to bed. We will have a proper family discussion in the morning. Come on, dear," he guided Simon's mum gently onto the couch and put a mug of tea in her hand.

Later Simon lay in bed. It felt strange to be falling asleep as the day got brighter and he heard his school pals passing on their way to catch the bus. His dad had tucked him in snugly and kissed him on the forehead, something he hadn't done for years.

"We'll talk in the morning," he said, and Simon felt secure.

He was awakened by the sound of whistling: someone whistling and making a lot of noise in the kitchen. Dad was home. The smell of sliced sausage grilling wafted into his room. Simon was ravenous. He tumbled out of bed straight downstairs to the kitchen.

His dad waved a fork at him. "Don't make a noise," he said. "Your mum's still sleeping. Want a roll and sausage?"

Simon poured a puddle of brown sauce on to his roll and bit into it, delicious!

"What time is it?"

"Nearly twelve o'clock. I've phoned the hospital. By the sound of things Jessica is creating havoc up there. I've phoned your Granny and Uncle John. They'll probably go over for afternoon visiting. Want another sausage?"

The two of them sat and ate their breakfast together.

"Simon," his dad said seriously. "Your mum and I had a long talk last night and with your help we are going to get this family going again. What do you say?"

"That's what I've been saying for months," said Simon. "It's just as Mr Peterson says, like Bruce and the spider, try again."

"Life is not as simple as that, Simon."

"I know," said Simon patiently. "It's a lot more involved and complicated, but we mustn't forget the basic fact that people have need of each other. Mrs Davies told us that."

"Oh, did she. What else was she saying?"

"It was the day after it was announced that the steel works would close down. She said redundancy was meant for things, not for human beings."

"I think we'll write that out in block capitals and pin it on the kitchen wall," said a voice.

They looked up. Mrs Ross was standing in the doorway.

Simon's dad made a flourish with the towel.

"Tea and toast, Madam?"

"Yes, please," said Simon's mother. She flopped down into a chair. "I'm shattered."

"Well the good news is that I've phoned the hospital and Jessica is much better. They said she might even be allowed home tomorrow."

17

Simon had a leisurely bath and put on some clothes. They went to the shops and bought some things for Jessica. Then they waited at the bus stop to catch the bus to the hospital. Mrs Boyce came along as they stood there.

"Was that an ambulance I saw at your house last night, Mrs Ross?"

"No," said Simon quietly. "It was a M4A6 American Sherman Tank."

"The baby's not very well, Mrs Boyce," said Simon's dad.

"I'm sorry to hear that. I suppose she caught a chill when she got drenched in all that rain on Saturday," she observed.

Simon's mother rolled her eyes.

"Thanks for your brilliant diagnosis. We'll let the doctors know when we reach the hospital," muttered Simon.

"Been travelling around?" she asked Simon's dad.

"Oh, here and there. Oh look, here comes the bus."

Simon's dad was laughing as they got on the bus. "Some things never change," he said.

"Let me know if you need any help," Mrs Boyce called after them. "Simon could always come to my house for his tea after school if that's any help."

"Over my dead body," said Simon as he sat down and put the stuffed rabbit he had bought Jessica down on the seat beside him.

"Now, now, she means well," said his mother.

"Hah! Hah!" said Simon. "That's not what you were saying on Saturday."

"That was then, this is now," said his mum primly.

They arrived at the hospital to find Granny and Uncle John already there. They were sitting on either side of the cot.

"Joe," said Granny, "it's good to see you, man."

"Aye, it's good to see you too," he said and kissed her smack on the mouth.

Jessica was round-eyed at all the presents. Simon disobeyed the rules and lifted her out of the cot. He took her over to the window and showed her the cars and trees outside.

Uncle John came over and murmured in his ear. "Did you manage to sort those two out?"

Simon glanced back to where his mum and dad and gran were sitting talking. Mum was telling Granny about the ambulance driver, while dad threw back his head and laughed.

Uncle John winked at him. "The ways of the Lord are mysterious," he said. He took Jessica's hand, "Unless ye become like children ...," he spread the plump little fingers against the side of his rough cheek.

Simon's mother decided to wait at the hospital and help to give Jessica her tea. "I want to ask if she might be discharged tomorrow."

The rest of the family went back to the Ross house.

"Simon," said his father, "would you like to run across for some chips and I'll put the kettle on and set the table."

Simon took the money and went towards the shops. He called in quickly at Mr Peterson's to tell him why he hadn't come after school. The shop was beginning to look slightly less chaotic.

"You hurry on now," said Mr Peterson. "Tell your dad I was asking after him. And give your mum and Jessica my love."

Simon and his dad washed up the dishes while Granny Campbell ironed some of Jessica's clothes for the morning.

"If she's coming home tomorrow she is going to look her best," she said as she spread a little pink dress over the back of a chair. A lump came into Simon's throat as he looked at it. It was so tiny, and he thought of the person who belonged to it spending another night in that vast hospital.

The door bell rang. It was Mr Boyce from the end of the road.

"Here, Joe," he said and handed Mr Ross his car keys. "That'll save you trailing around and waiting for buses."

"Oh, no. I couldn't really ..." Simon's dad started to say.

"Thanks very much," said Simon quickly, taking the keys from Mr Boyce's hand.

"Simon!" said his father after Mr Boyce had gone.

"I was thinking of Granny," said Simon. "It will save her legs, and it will mean we don't have to talk to Mrs Boyce every time we go for a bus. Anyway, Mrs Davies said you mustn't be too proud to take things. You must allow people to give — it makes them feel good."

"Oh, well in that case ..." said his dad.

At evening visiting Jessica was back to her old self.

"This child's exhausting me," said Mrs Ross. "The nurses will be glad to get rid of her tomorrow."

"Is it definite that she will get home?" asked Simon.

"We'll find out in the morning after the doctor has done his rounds, but it is almost certain. Look at her!"

Jessica was bouncing up and down in the cot with excitement. She was playing a game which involved throwing the stuffed rabbit that Simon had given her as far across the ward as possible, and Simon had to go and fetch it for her. He bounced it off her head. After a while Jessica settled down and eventually Simon's mum got her to sleep.

Everyone was very quiet as they got into Mr Boyce's car to go home. Simon's mum wiped away a tear, Simon's dad put his arm around her shoulder. They drove Granny and Great Uncle John home first.

"I'll phone you tomorrow," said Simon's mother.

"I think I'll go to bed," she said as they returned to their own house.

"I'll bring you up a cup of tea and then maybe Simon and I will go for a walk. Would you like that, Simon?" said his dad as he went through to the kitchen.

They left the house and walked through the cool evening. Simon knew instinctively where they were going. They took a path which led up behind the precinct and came out onto the canal towpath. It was a walk they had often taken together in the past. The hills made a soft blur in the distance. The sky above them was gold and green as the last rays of the sun reached out long fingers of light. Small nocturnal animals made rustling noises and the trees whispered above their heads as they strolled along, no conversation necessary. Simon breathed in deeply.

"This is a lovely part of the world," said his dad, "despite everything."

"Are we going to stay here?" asked Simon.

"If we possibly can," his father replied. "I am going to have to sit down and work out some kind of a plan, but we will all do it together." He stopped and leaned against the trunk of a tree. From here the land sloped gently away to their right and at the base of the incline lay the steel mill. Machinery was already being sold off and a crane stood like a great predatory bird outlined against the night sky.

His father looked out over the grey desolate scene without saying a word. Once huge coils of steel had been stacked here awaiting despatch to places like Essen and Antwerp, and huge transport lorries had come and gone, giving the place a vitality of its own.

"It was more than a job," his father said suddenly. "When I was young, when you started work people used the expression 'earning your livelihood.' That is what it was for me, my livelihood. My life. I was part of it, it was part of me. And now it's over."

Simon moved close to his father.

"I suppose it's a bit like Great-Uncle John in the war," he said. "If you hurt inside it takes you much longer to recover."

His father looked down at him.

"That about sums it up, Simon. You know when the war was on, and the men were away, the women worked as crane drivers and mill operators. Your Granny Ross was a helmet hand. She used to say she had made the helmet your grandad was wearing on D-Day. The mill turned out thousands of steel square which were sent to Sheffield to be made into helmets. The women got paid about two pounds a week and a free pint of milk if they were on the squad that had to use lead paint on the Nissen hut iron. I've got a picture of her somewhere in her blue boiler suit."

In the pale rising moonlight the buildings were clearly visible.

"The mill never suffered a hit though there were plenty of air raids," his father went on. "Mind you, the shipyards got it all right."

On a night like this the enemy planes could follow

the glittering ribbon of the Clyde and find their targets easily. He looked up into the sky.

"A real bombers' moon tonight," he said.

Simon looked up. "There's the Plough," he said, "and the Great Bear." He stopped.

And suddenly he remembered. He knew why the thief who had stolen Mr Peterson's computers last Thursday had bumped into him. It was because, he, Simon had been standing looking up at the stars. And he remembered with blinding clarity what had prompted him to do that. Now he had the last piece of the jigsaw. He had the answer!

18

Simon gripped his father's arm.

"Dad, Dad, I've remembered," he shouted.

"What?"

"On Thursday night," said Simon, in a voice trembling with excitement. "I was standing doing what I am doing now — looking up at the stars. And I didn't see the thief coming towards me. That's why he bumped into me!"

"Is that important?" asked his father.

"Yes," said Simon, "yes, because the reason I was looking up at the stars was that I had just read the number plate on the van! It read SKY. That is what made me look up into the sky. See?"

"You mean you actually know the registration letters of the van which was used in the robbery?"

"Yes, yes, yes," shouted Simon.

"That's incredible."

"I knew there was something else that I had to remember," said Simon.

"What about the numbers?" asked his father. "Can you recall any of those?"

"There was a five and a nine but I don't know the rest."

"I should think that's quite enough. We'll need to let the police know right away."

They walked home together, Simon running ahead occasionally, and doubling back to speak to his dad every few minutes. He told his father everything that had been happening at school and his experience at the mill when the cats were being killed. His father told him that one or two of the men had taken some of the tamer cats home with them on their last day at work. "We knew something like that was going to happen," he said. "Some of the older cats were very tame. We had names for them."

Simon told him about Killer.

His father laughed. "I don't think it will get a chance to kill anything at Gerry's house," he said. "How is his dad, by the way?"

"The same as ever," said Simon.

"I must go over and see him soon," said Mr Ross.

When they got back home they telephoned the police station at once. The desk officer said he would try to contact Detective Inspector Harrison and that he would no doubt be in touch.

Simon made some hot chocolate. It was getting late and he hadn't had much sleep over the last twenty-four hours but he was not the least bit tired. His mind was wide awake and alert.

The phone rang around half past ten. His father answered it quickly in case it woke Simon's mum. He spoke for a few minutes and then put the phone down.

"That was Detective Inspector Harrison," he said. "He's going to come along here tonight and have a chat with you. Then he'll take you into Headquarters and run your information through the main computer. That is, if you feel up to it," he added.

"Oh yes," said Simon, "yes please."

Simon was ready and waiting when eventually Detective Inspector Harrison arrived.

He shook hands with Mr Ross.

"Bright boy you've got there," he said, "but don't worry, I'll return him safe and well."

They drove quickly through the night to Divisional

Headquarters. Detective Inspector Harrison showed his pass and signed Simon in.

"We are going into a special security section tonight," he said.

They walked along brightly lit corridors until they came to a special room where they had to show their passes.

"This is part of our main computer. Here we can link up with the rest of Britain," said Detective Inspector Harrison. "We have access to all computerized criminal records held in Britain and a lot more besides."

"How does it all work?" asked Simon.

"Haven't a clue," came the cheerful reply. "We rely on these chaps here to press all the right buttons," and he waved towards some men who were sitting at desks around the room.

"Do people work here all night?" asked Simon.

"There is usually a night shift of one or two to cover any emergency."

"Like a terrorist attack or a national disaster?"

"Shrewd thinking, Simon. Exactly. However, it's not going to be a disaster tonight, is it?"

They went over to one of the desks and sat down. It had a larger screen than the other desks had, and the operator's name was Peter.

"Right," he said, "what have you got and what do you want?"

"We've got part of a licence number and we want to know the location of the van it belongs to."

"Just like that?"

"Just like that."

Peter keyed in their information and then another coding and sat back and waited.

"Actually this bit is pretty boring," he said. "The

machine is doing all the work." After a minute or two something came up on the screen.

"That means," said Peter, "that the number does not belong to any vehicle registered as stolen anywhere in Britain."

"How up to date is that?" asked Simon.

"To within the last five seconds of anything being registered as stolen."

"Whew."

Working like this they covered any computerized transactions involving motor cars, including sales, transfer of number plates, or vehicles involved in an accident. They drew a blank each time.

"Have you any information at all as to its location within the last week?" asked Peter.

"Yes," said Simon. "We know it was in Glenburn on Thursday night."

Peter flicked a switch and an Ordnance Survey map appeared on the screen. "We have scanners on some of these motorways," he said, "and perhaps your friend travelled on one of them round about last Thursday."

"Why don't you link into the National Vehicle Registration Centre?" said Simon suddenly.

"I was wondering when you were going to ask me that," said Peter. "Because your vehicle is an old model; I can tell by the number. At the time it was registered the files weren't computerized, and no retrospective work has been done yet. Aha!" he said. "What have we here?"

Simon looked and there flashing on the screen was a car number:

SKY 659 E

And Simon knew without a shadow of doubt that it belonged to the van he had seen parked at the precinct last Thursday night.

19

"That's it!" he cried. "I'm sure of it."

"Now just wait a minute until we establish where this came from exactly," said Peter.

"Got it. That number is from a scanner on a bridge at a bypass twelve miles south of Glenburn, day Thursday, time 18:00 hours, vehicle travelling on the northbound carriageway."

"Bingo!" said Detective Inspector Harrison jubilantly.

"I can do even better than that," said Peter. "That area is a notorious accident black spot. We might have him on film. Let me check the code number. Yes, we have last week's film right here in HQ. It will only take a few minutes to have it sent up."

While he was talking, Peter was pressing other keys on the machine.

"Look," he said suddenly. "There he is again."

"Can you give us a reading on that location?" asked Simon.

"That one's from the scanner on the City Bridge in Glasgow," and he added softly, "it was taken less than fifteen minutes ago."

Simon had never seen Detective Inspector Harrison move so quickly before. He flashed across the room to where a green telephone was fixed on the wall and dialled a number.

He spoke quickly. "Detective Inspector Harrison, Glenburn Division, assisting in Operation Download. I have information requiring immediate action. A van believed to have been involved in the Glenburn raid has been sighed crossing the City Bridge only fifteen minutes ago on its way into the centre of Glasgow." He listened for a minute or two, then he gave the licence number and the description. He hung up and came back over to the computer desk.

"You've been a great help," he said to Peter. "I'm going down to Special Operations. Would you send the film of the van down there, please, when it comes?" He turned to Simon. "Want to come?"

"Oh yes, please," said Simon.

Whereas the Computer Room had been quiet save for the humming noise given off by tapes running, the Special Operations Room seemed full of people. They went across to a dais where a large florid man sat in his shirt sleeves.

"Hello, Harrison," he said. "We've been chasing these blighters for months and it takes an eleven-year-old boy to come up with our best clue. You must be Simon," he said, and without pausing to give Simon time to answer he went on. "We've got the city ringed. I tell you, whatever job he's pulling tonight it's his last. He's not getting away with anything else on my patch."

Simon looked round the room. The noise was incredible. There were operators at a dozen or so stations sitting on swivel chairs. They were wearing headsets and talking continuously into their microphones. Above them along one wall were television screens showing traffic movement in different parts of the city.

The Detective Chief Inspector in charge came round and shook Simon's hand.

"I'm Bill Smith," he said, "and I can tell you I'm pleased to see you and glad that you've got a good memory. The police in the Midlands and the North of England are going to be grateful to you, I can tell you. He's been a thorn in their flesh. Specialist, you see,

only goes for certain stuff. Hah well, I am going for him
tonight. That's why he went for your friend Mr
Peterson; his equipment is a little out of the ordinary
— he modifies it, you know. We think that's how our
thief knows which shops to hit. He must have a way of
knowing who buys specialist parts; maybe he is a sales
rep or works for a supplier. We'd have got him that
way, you know, eventually. Good solid police work, sort-
ing through files, checking and rechecking. Policeman
Plod stuff. But then we didn't have to, did we? We had
you, eh?"

He was worse than Mrs Boyce, thought Simon. At
least she stopped occasionally.

Detective Chief Inspector Smith was back behind his
operations table rifling through papers. "We are going
to have to be very careful with this chappie," he said.
"He's nobody's fool. The way he dismantled the burglar alarms on each of the premises he had broken into
proves that. Your boys ready for action if need be,
Harrison?"

"Ready and waiting, sir."

"Good, good." Detective Chief Inspector Smith got
up and studied a large map of the city which covered
one whole wall of the Operations Room. He was
whistling cheerfully.

Simon's head was whirling. "Don't be fooled by all
that chatter," said Detective Inspector Harrison in his
ear. "He is an extremely efficient person."

The film of last Thursday's traffic south of Glenburn
arrived and was switched onto one of the TV monitors.
A digital read-out of the time of day was running in one
corner so that they knew when the van would come
into sight. As the clock neared 6 pm Simon felt his
stomach contract. A white object was approaching,
only a blur in the distance, and then it filled the screen

and was past all in a matter of seconds. They ran it back in slow motion. This time they could see the van driver's face quite clearly, and Simon noticed at once he was wearing a green parka.

"It's him!" shouted Simon.

Detective Chief Inspector Smith clapped him on the back. "A positive identification. Mind you, we'll need more evidence than that, but don't worry, we'll get it tonight."

They put the van driver's face on freeze frame and circulated his description to all the police units who were prowling the city of Glasgow. Simon looked at him closely. He didn't look like a desperate criminal; he just looked like an ordinary person.

It wasn't long after that a report came in from a police car on the south side of the city. The suspect had been spotted. They awaited instructions.

20

Detective Inspector Harrison leapt to his feet.

"Instruct them to stay well back," said Detective Chief Inspector Smith. "Well back," he repeated. "Right, Harrison, get your show on the road."

Detective Inspector Harrison made to leave the room, and then he hesitated and looked at Simon.

Detective Chief Inspector Smith looked at Simon.

"OK," he said, "but for goodness sake look after him. And you," he addressed Simon. "Do *exactly* as you're told."

"Yes, *sir*," said Simon.

They drove quickly in an unmarked car to where the last sighting had been.

"Where are the rest of your men?" asked Simon.

"Oh they're around," was the rather vague reply.

They stopped several streets away from the warehouse near which the van was parked. They gained access to the roof of a nearby block of flats using a key which Detective Inspector Harrison had brought with him.

"How did you happen to have the key that fits this door with you?" said Simon.

The detective pulled a key ring with about sixty different keys on it from his pocket.

"One for every occasion," he said.

He handed Simon a pair of binoculars. Simon watched very closely. He scanned the yard area, the car park, the roof opposite. He could see nothing. Suddenly he stiffened with alarm. An old down-and-out was staggering across the yard. The tramp had his head down muttering to himself and he clutched

a bottle to his chest. He was going to ruin everything. Simon signalled to Detective Inspector
Harrison.

"Look," he whispered. "Look."

Detective Inspector Harrison looked down into the
yard.

"Hare in position, hare in position," he spoke into
a radio handset.

There was a crackle and then the reply,
"Information received and understood."

Simon saw the tramp sit down against a wall.

"He is one of ours," said Detective Inspector
Harrison.

They waited. Nothing happened. Simon began to
get impatient and then to worry. Supposing the thief
had been and gone and they had missed him. Had he
got out a back way.

As if he knew what he was thinking Detective
Inspector Harrison whispered in his ear. "This is the
worst part, waiting, not knowing if he is still in there
or not."

Simon surveyed the building again. Would he come
out via the roof? Where would an electronic expert
break in — someone who could dismantle sophisticated burglar alarms? What would his point of entry
and exit be? Now that he thought about it, the
answer was obvious. Simon lowered his binoculars
until they focused on the warehouse door. And even
as he did so he saw it very slowly begin to open.

He started to say something but Detective
Inspector Harrison gripped his arm. He spoke into
his radio.

"One," he said.

There was no reply.

The man advanced cautiously. He was carrying

only a small box. Simon was to learn later that it was worth many thousands of pounds. He walked across the car park, keeping to the shadows. The tramp did not move.

"Two."

The man stopped and looked around him. Everything was quiet and empty but he was suspicious. Some sixth sense told him that all was not as it should be. Would he run back to the warehouse where they might lose him?

He made up his mind. He moved forwards towards the gate and freedom.

"THREE," said Detective Inspector Harrison. And in the next instant everything happened at once. A police car, headlights blazing, swept through the gates; the tramp raced across the yard and put an armlock on the thief, and several plain-clothes policemen seemed to appear from nowhere. They radioed HQ.

Detective Inspector Harrison allowed Simon to make the call.

"Mission successfully accomplished," said Simon.

They went back to Special Operations to make a report.

"Well done, good work," said Detective Chief Inspector Smith.

"I'll do a full report later," said Detective Inspector Harrison. "And I'll certainly be seeing you in the very near future," he said to Simon as he dropped him off home.

He waited and exchanged a few words with Simon's father.

"Simon will fill you in on the details, but it is absolutely certain that this case would not have been wound up so quickly if your son hadn't helped us."

Simon kept thinking about these words as he lay in bed trying to sleep.

"You get some sleep," said his father when he came in to say goodnight. "Remember, Jessica will probably be home tomorrow and we will need all our energy."

21

Simon woke late the next morning, and lay in bed trying to remember what day of the week it was. He could hardly believe it was only Wednesday — he felt as though he hadn't been to school for at least a week. He got dressed slowly and went downstairs. His mother was in the kitchen, humming happily as she peeled some potatoes.

"What are you so cheerful about?" said Simon and yawned.

"Jessica is coming home today. We'll go and collect her when your dad gets back."

"Where *is* dad?"

"He's gone to the shops. He told me that you single-handedly rounded up a gang of criminals last night."

"That's an exaggeration, it was one man and I was miles away."

"Well, anyway, I thought you would be more excited about it. I hope you're not sickening for something."

Simon poured some cereal into a plate. "It's a bit of a let-down this morning. I don't know why. It was great last night but now I feel sorry for the thief."

"Don't feel sorry for him, feel sorry for Mr Peterson and all those other people he stole from. He nearly ruined Mr Peterson's whole life."

"Yeh, I suppose so," Simon began to spoon cereal slowly into his mouth.

"Gerry and Guthrie called in on their way to school. Guthrie was sure you had been kidnapped."

"He would be."

"They are going to call round after tea, and I've been waiting until you are fully awake before I told you this.

The local newspaper called. They want to interview you."

"The *Glenburn Gazette*? Me?"

"Yes. They heard about your part in solving the robbery and they want to come round and take your picture."

Simon considered this. He would have to check with Detective Inspector Harrison — he didn't want to prejudice any evidence he might be required to give later. He would emphasize the part that computers played. That might be useful later on when he was talking to his parents about buying him one. He would also take the opportunity to give Mr Peterson's shop a free plug. He thought of a sentence in which the word "Peterson's" occurred more than three times. "On my way home last Thursday as I was passing Peterson's Electronics Shop, I happened to notice, outside Peterson's, a van parked, the driver of which appeared to be loading goods into Peterson's shop." That would do nicely.

"Simon, wake up," his mother said. "You're miles away."

Mr Ross returned from the shops. He had brought Granny Campbell and Great-Uncle John with him.

"I thought we might as well have a reception committee for her ladyship returning," he said.

Simon and his parents set off for the hospital. As they passed the end of the road Mrs Boyce waved to them from her garden. Simon waved back and smiled. It was a lovely day.

Simon and his dad waited in the waiting room while Mrs Ross got Jessica dressed in the ward and collected her things. Simon looked around him. He remembered the last time he had been here. He shuddered. Jessica came out clutching her stuffed rabbit. She managed a few steps before starting to teeter about. Simon got up and grabbed her. He swung her high into the air.

"Welcome home," he said and buried his face in her neck.

Mr Ross went to return the car to Mrs Boyce, and Granny sat Jessica on her knee and played with her in the living room. Simon went into the kitchen to help his mum. He looked out of the back window. Great-Uncle John had gone into the garden to try to salvage some of Simon's dad's attempts at vegetable growing. He was now attempting to have a conversation with Mrs McPhee across the back fence. Simon grinned. The two of them would get on terrifically, he thought.

His father returned from the Boyce's house an hour later.

"That's it," he said. "We're buying another car. I'm not going through that again. The police should recruit her to interrogate people."

They all sat down to dinner. Jessica sat in her high chair and got titbits from nearly everybody's plate. She was soon yawning her head off.

"Bed," said Mrs Ross firmly, "and," she added, "you too, Simon."

22

A few weeks later Mr Peterson held the official reopening of his shop. A reporter from the *Glenburn Gazette* was there (Simon had convinced him when he gave his interview that it was an occasion not to be missed). The shop looked tremendous. Simon and Mr Peterson had worked really hard, helped sometimes but mainly hindered by Gerry and Guthrie. Mr Peterson had cut the article on Simon out of the paper and stuck it up behind the counter. Simon's face smiled out from the picture. He particularly like the bit which read, "This intelligent and quick-witted local boy deserves full marks for observation and presence of mind ..."

There were lots of people there, milling about, sipping drinks and chatting. Jessica was tottering around in her new shoes. Simon slipped her some crisps.

Mr Peterson clapped his hands.

"Simon," he said. "I would like you to declare the shop officially open."

"I declare this shop officially open," said Simon.

Everyone cheered loudly.

"And," Mr Peterson went on, "I have another announcement to make. Would Detective Inspector Harrison please step forward?"

Simon looked up. He hadn't known that Detective Inspector Harrison was here this evening.

"Over to you, Detective Inspector," said Mr Peterson.

"Simon, come over here and stand beside me," said Detective Inspector Harrison.

Simon crossed the room.

"Simon," began Detective Inspector Harrison,

"without you this particular series of crimes, which had been puzzling police both north and south of the border, would have taken very much longer to solve. And as a token of our appreciation, and helped by the store owners whose stock you helped to recover, we should like to present you with this." He lifted a box out from under the counter.

Simon knew before he opened it what was inside. It was a computer. And not just any computer. It was one of the most sophisticated models money could buy.

His face went very red.

"Thank you very much," he said.

Everybody cheered again.

His mother came over. "I'm really interested in how this thing is going to improve the quality of my life," she said. "Later, later," she added hurriedly as Simon started to take some packaging out of the box.

His father came up. "You will need to teach me how those things work, son," he said peering into the box.

Simon lifted Jessica up and sat her on top of the box.

"Mustn't leave you out," he said. "From now on we do everything together in this family."

New School Blues

Theresa Breslin

Two pupils from different primary schools meet up to cause mayhem in this very funny book about moving up from Primary to Secondary School.

Despite strict instructions from her over-protective parents to behave, Mary McPherson finds that her new classmate, Jamie, has no intention of keeping to the rules. A ferocious bull, an angry farmer, a dispute over a right of way and an old gravekeeper all combine to cause them lots of parent and teacher trouble.

For more information, book notes and activities check out **www.theresabreslin.com**

Kelpies

Different Directions

Theresa Breslin

No one should have to help their own mother with her maths homework!

Okay, so Katharine's mother wants to go back to school but did she have to choose *her* school? Her friends all think Mrs Douglas is great, but Katharine feels embarrassed, especially when she hears rumours about her mother and Hedgehog, the maths teacher. As if she hasn't got enough problems of her own!

But then Katharine learns something about her mother which puts everything else into perspective, and unexpectedly brings them closer together.

For more information, book notes and activities check out **www.theresabreslin.com**

Kelpies